Camilla Isley is an engineer t
job to follow her husband on a
She's a cat lover, coffee addi
writing, she loves reading—duh!—cooking, watching bad TV, and going to the movies—popcorn, please. She's a bit of a foodie, nothing too serious.

A keen traveler, Camilla knows mosquitoes play a role in the ecosystem, and she doesn't want to starve all those frog princes out there, but she could really live without them.

You can find out more about her here: **www.camillaisley.com** and by following her on Instagram or Facebook.

@camillaisley
facebook.com/camillaisley

By the Same Author

Romantic Comedies

Stand Alones

I Wish for You
A Sudden Crush

First Comes Love Series

Love Connection
Opposites Attract
I Have Never
A Christmas Date
To the Stars and Back
From Thailand with Love
You May Kiss the Bridesmaid
Sweet Love and Country Roads

Christmas Romantic Comedy Series

Fool Me Twice at Christmas
A Christmas Caroline
Home for Christmas

New Adult College Romance

Just Friends Series

Let's Be Just Friends
Friend Zone
My Best Friend's Boyfriend
I Don't Want To Be Friends

CAMILLA ISLEY

Fool Me Twice

Christmas Romantic Comedy Book 1

This is a work of fiction. Names, characters, businesses, places, events and incidents either are products of the author's imagination or are used fictitiously. Any resemblance to actual events or locales or persons, living or dead, is entirely coincidental.

ISBN-13: 978-8887269581

Dedication

To chocolate and all chocolate lovers…

One

Chuck

What a beautiful, crappy day. The sun shines on a gloriously snow-lined Interstate 75 in staggering contrast to my stormy mood. On a regular day, I wouldn't particularly enjoy driving for hours—I get motion-sick pretty easily, even if I'm at the wheel. But today I'd trade a limb, or possibly even a minor, non-vital organ, to be anywhere other than stuck in a rental car with my ex-girlfriend-turned-fake-girlfriend as we head home for the holidays.

I tap my fingertips on the steering wheel and throw a glance at the emerald numbers of the car's digital clock—*and we've still got two hours of sunny road ahead! Joy of joys.*

Kate and I started fighting the moment I pulled up in front of our old apartment in Ann Arbor at noon to pick her up. Too late, in her opinion. A wasted half day. A totally reasonable hour for me, considering I had to pack, grab a bite to eat before the long journey, and walk to the rental office to collect the car, which of course wasn't the right model. Toy-size, according to Kate; perfectly proportioned, according to me. Then, we argued about the dimensions of her luggage—exaggerated in my eyes, essential in hers—which also explained why she considered the car too small.

"I have presents to bring home," she argued. "Didn't you buy any?"

And when I said I planned to do my Christmas shopping in Bluewater Springs, she gave a theatrical eye roll. "Of course, why would you put some thought and care in choosing gifts for your loved ones? Do it last minute, like always. It's your specialty."

To which I didn't respond.

But the bickering isn't why we're sitting so tensely in this overstuffed Nissan Versa we risk snapping in half at every bump on the road. No, we're on pins and needles because, for the past four months, we've barely been in each other's lives. Definitely not in person. Definitely not for hours at a time. And definitely not in such a confined space like the passenger compartment of a—*allegedly tiny*—car.

Until today, our sole communications since the end of summer break amounted to the odd, informational text about momentous happenings in our days the other should be aware of to keep up the farce. As relationships go, ours grew nice and steady over the years as we progressed from best friends to dating to living together, but then crashed alarmingly fast on the way down—a falling, vertical smear of a breakup that flat-lined into this fake-relationship sham we're now carrying out for the sake of our families.

Anyway, now that she's run out of criticisms, Kate is giving me the silent treatment. Which she knows I hate.

Silence is uncomfortable.

Angry silence is unbearable.

When I can't stand the bitter muteness any longer, I give up and ask a question on the only topic that still unites us. "How do you want to tell them?"

Kate, who's been pointedly staring out the window, her big brown eyes unwilling to meet mine even for a glimpse, turns on me. "Since *you're* telling them, you can do it however you choose."

I frown. "Why should *I* be the one to tell our parents?"

"Because it's all your fault."

"If I remember correctly, you dumped me. So, if anyone should take the blame, it's you."

Kate pulls a lock of her chestnut hair behind her ear and crosses her arms over her chest. "Not when you didn't leave me any choice, with you being such an immature—"

"Save it," I interrupt, staring at the straight, infinite road ahead. "I don't care to listen to a list of my shortcomings again. And I sure won't stand in front of the firing squad alone. I wouldn't even know what to tell them."

"Go with the truth. It's always the best approach."

"Which would be?"

"That we don't love each other anymore."

Ah.

My mouth parches as I remember the day she informed me of this fact. Needless to say, Kate's decision to end things between us totally blindsided me. A sudden breakup with no chance of an appeal after a romance that had lasted almost a decade came to me as a real shock. A freezing-cold shower.

And, okay, maybe I wasn't grand-gesturing her every other day, and I might've taken our relationship a little too much for granted. I'm man enough to admit that. But I'd always assumed we'd grow old together. She was my rock, and I was hers. Full stop.

Only, she had different plans. Plans that involved a new, shinier, half-Cuban rock.

No, she didn't cheat on me, I'm positive. Kate just moved on painfully and humiliatingly fast. I don't know the details—I haven't asked—but we still have enough friends in common for the news to reach me that she has a new boyfriend. Marco Guerra.

His Instagram account, where he delights his followers with daily sweaty videos of himself working out at the gym, has given me enough insight into this guy's life to know he's the complete opposite of my nerdy, computer-rat self.

Marco is a stud, but, other than that, what do they talk about when they're together? How many pounds he can bench press?

Admittedly, the dude's not all brawn. He must have some brain, considering he teaches Latin American and Caribbean Art to undergrads at the University of Michigan. That must be it: his knowledge of the arts provides him enough savoir faire and catchphrases to hoodwink women. Kate must feel oh-so-sophisticated for dating a professor.

I keep my focus on the road ahead and don't contradict her declaration that our love is over. Instead, I move on to the last practical step needed to put an official end to my first and *only* relationship: how to tell our families.

It would have been easier if our parents were just old friends who'd always dreamed about their offspring getting married and merging the bloodlines. But no, the Warrens and the Roses do nothing in half measures. Our parents are not only the best of friends, but also business partners and co-owners, with a twenty-five percent share each, of The Bluewater Springs Chocolate Company.

Bluewater Springs is renowned in America for exactly two things: our stunning fall foliage, and our delicious chocolates. The factory is the only industry in our hometown, a small village on Lake Michigan about fifteen minutes north of Traverse City, which makes us basically celebrities there. Big fish in a small pond, as that notoriety doesn't extend much past the town's borders.

Our parents founded the business as newlyweds fresh out of college, and they've grown the organization for thirty years, turning The Bluewater Springs Chocolate Company into an international corporation that distributes to over forty countries worldwide.

But the company isn't just a business for us; it's a dream we all share and want to keep expanding moving forward. My very first memories growing up are within the factory halls, back when both our families used to live in the twin attic apartments above the original production facilities. The apartments no longer exist, and have long since been turned into office spaces, but my entire childhood is crammed into that building.

But I digress. The main side effect of our parents' success and unbreakable friendship is the way they've been invested in my relationship with Kate since we started dating in high school.

Now that I think about it, the familial pressure probably didn't help us make things work. It might have even been a wedge driving us apart. The sense of entrapment. The obligations and expectations that our parents and the town put on us as heirs to the chocolate kingdom. And the unwillingness we had to disappoint them.

I sigh, trying to find some middle ground, now, between us. "Why don't I tell my mom and dad, and you tell yours?" I propose. "It's only fair."

Kate pouts in that way that is not a 'yes,' but not a definite 'no' either. I'll mark it down as a victory and interpret her silence as tacit consent.

A small triumph.

So why do I still feel like the biggest loser?

Two

Kate

Frozen gravel crunches under the tires as Chuck pulls up in front of my parents' house. The sky should be dark at five p.m. in the dead of winter, but the snow blanketing the garden amplifies the porch lamps and the light streaming through the windows, creating a daylight illusion that brightens the night with a widespread yellow glow.

Chuck kills the engine and turns to me with a heavy sigh. All he does lately is sigh. He's been doing it nonstop for the past four hours, and I'm already fed up with him constantly playing the martyr. I pulled the trigger on us, true, but our relationship had been crumbling for months when I called it quits. It was only waiting for someone to bring it behind the barn and shoot it. And that person had to be me, same as for everything else in our lives.

Decide where to go on vacation? *Kate, you pick, I'm fine with whatever you choose.*

Book the hotel? *Kate, you know you're better at this stuff than I am. If I do it, we'd just end up in a dump or paying double.*

Go out to dinner? *Kate, I don't care what we eat, whatever works.*

He didn't bat a lash even when I brought him to a hard-core vegan restaurant that served only raw foods and kombucha-fermented cocktails. I was trying to shake things up. Not that he noticed.

Chuck, would you rather play the latest Final Fantasy three millionth game, or the new Halo?

Now, *that* would open up a debate.

I can't even remember a time when he didn't pay more attention to his stupid PlayStation than me.

Once, I even tried that silly drop-the-towel internet challenge to grab his attention. I snuck up on him while he was playing, dropped my towel to the floor, and sauntered to the bathroom naked, saying, "I'm going to take a shower."

Chuck kept pushing buttons on his stupid controller, eyes glued to the screen. "Yeah, yeah, Honey. Later."

What question he thought he was answering, I'll never know. But if I needed any more proof we were over, that was it. Still, it was easier to stick to my I've-made-the-right-choice convictions when I didn't have to see him or be so close to him that I can smell his aftershave—a sensual, oriental, woody seduction elixir I've never been able to resist. Same as I haven't been able to resist his deep blue eyes or midnight black hair ever since hitting puberty. Chuck is hot in a goofy, skinny, nerdy kind of way. And, apparently, four months apart haven't immunized me. *Yet.* But I'll get there in time.

"I guess I'll help you unload your stuff," Chuck says, turning his head toward the over-packed back of the car that took us an hour to sandwich together in a real-life Tetris game. "Then go home to see my parents." Another sigh. Good thing he keeps annoying me with all the sighing; otherwise, I'd be losing my mind—and my will to keep him in the past—right now. "When do you want to toss the grenade?"

"Right away," I say without hesitation. "The sooner we can stop lying, the better."

We started the ruse back in September because we thought the shock would be lessened if we told our parents in person—then chickened out and skipped on Thanksgiving to avoid facing them. But now that we're finally here, I'm starting to wish we'd just texted them four months ago and gotten it over with. Anyway, no point crying over spilled chocolate, this is the last push and the nightmare will be over.

"You want to tell them *now?*" Chuck protests. As always, we're on completely different wavelengths. "Kate, I'm tired. I just drove four hours. Can't we give it a rest, at least for tonight?"

"No. Waiting will only make things harder. I say we go in there and rip the Band-Aid—"

"THEY'RE HERE!" A scream rips through the night, cutting me off.

My mom runs down the porch steps in her pink Uggs, a white wool cardigan wrapped tightly around her shoulders to shield her against the winter wind. Dad follows close on her heels. Then Chuck's mom and dad, too.

Ah, a full welcome committee! We should've known.

Chuck and I have barely exited the car when the parents descend upon us. The dads kiss us briefly before unloading the Nissan. The moms hug us and fuss.

"How was the journey?"

"We were expecting you hours ago!"

"You look tired, is everything okay?"

"Come, come inside, it's freezing out here."

The questions come in such a whirlwind I can't tell which mom asks what or who hugs me tighter.

I'm carried into the house on a tidal wave of more kisses, squeezes, and jostled suitcases, and wash ashore in the living room. Logs crackle in the fireplace, warming the main room of my parents' cabin-like home—a nice contrast to the chill of the outdoors.

My pops, Teddy, and Chuck's nana, Fern, are also waiting for us inside. The elderly are more restrained in their welcomes, mostly because old age doesn't allow them to grab us as quickly or forcefully as our parents, but the enthusiasm is just as boisterous. We've only been away for a few months, but they all act like we're soldiers coming back from the front.

Admittedly, us skipping Thanksgiving was an unprecedented act. We justified our absence inventing a fake romantic trip to Niagara Falls.

I went with Marco.

I don't know what Chuck did. Probably took part in a virtual fried turkey competition on his PlayStation.

But our absence must've been felt more than we imagined.

While Mom puts the finishing touches on dinner, the rest of us scatter across the living room.

At once, I'm bombarded with the usual million coming-back-home questions. How's school? How did you do on your finals? Are you eating enough? Did you lose weight, dear?

Chuck's nana always asks me if I've lost weight, but this time I've actually shed a few pounds since Marco convinced me to pick up running. Nana Fern probably wouldn't approve. She's already saddled with a skimpy grandson, and I've always been her chubby consolation prize.

But, thankfully, I don't have to admit the slim sin to Nana Fern as Mom comes into the room clapping to get our attention. "Come, everyone, sit down, dinner is ready."

I take a deep breath. Maybe having both families under the same roof isn't a bad thing. We can break the news to them all at once. And, this way, I'll also be able to control the narrative so Chuck can't portray me as a heartless bitch who dumped him for no reason.

I give my ex-boyfriend a loaded nod, then follow the others into the dining room.

The rectangular table is laid for eight, with three plates on each of the long sides and the other two at the near end. An honorific spot for me and Chuck, I assume. At the opposite end of the table, a lumpy shape covered in a deep-burgundy satin veil looms over the room.

"What's that?" I ask no one in particular.

"A surprise," Abigail, Chuck's mom, replies as she squeezes my hand.

"Ah."

Sounds ominous.

"Sit, sit," my mom urges as she disappears into the kitchen.

She comes back a minute later, holding a dish in each hand. Turkey casserole for Chuck, and the Warren family secret recipe meatloaf for me.

"Your favorite, Love." She places the casserole in front of Chuck and the meatloaf before me. "And yours also, Honeybun."

She disappears into the kitchen again and is soon back with a tray of Duck à l'Orange. She's cooked three ducks in total, all perfectly crispy and honey-gold glazed. See, my mom is a brilliant chef, and she's found her cooking soulmate in Chuck's dad. Mom and Bud are head chocolatiers at The Bluewater Springs Chocolate Company, while my dad and Abigail are in charge of the business side of things. Finance, Dad, and marketing, Chuck's mom. The four of them together are a perfect partnership, both in the professional sphere and in their personal lives as spouses and best friends.

And they have so many hopes pinned on Chuck and me and our relationship that I'm sure tonight's revelation will break their hearts. But the charade has to end. Now. The constant lying has drained me, and I don't want to lead them on anymore.

When all bellies are full, I nudge Chuck under the table with a knee and clear my throat. Since no one notices my attempt to speak, I stand up and clink my fork on my glass until everyone quiets down.

"Can I have everyone's attention for a minute, please? Chuck and I would like to make an announcement."

The moms exchange a complicit stare while Nana Fern places a hand over her heart. Oh, gosh, now they're probably expecting us to announce we're getting married.

Wrong move, Kate.

Much as I hate to admit it, Chuck was right. We should've broken the news to them separately—divide and conquer. Well, no turning back now.

"We… we…" Sweat pools under my armpits, and I swallow. I beckon Chuck to stand up next to me, and when he doesn't, I kick him under the table until he joins me.

"Wait!" my dad shouts, jumping to his feet. "Let me go get the champagne."

Before I can stop him, he rushes into the kitchen and comes back with a magnum bottle of bubbly in his hands. But as he excitedly walks past the lumpy shape near the door, fidgeting to remove the metal cage covering the champagne cork, the wire catches on the mystery object, pulling off the covering to reveal…

I gasp in horror at the life-sized standee of me and Chuck. In the photo, we're looking into each other's eyes, smiling, clearly head over heels in love.

"What's that?" Chuck asks, sounding as shocked as I feel.

Abigail playfully swats my dad's arm. "You've ruined the surprise, Mick." Then, pointing at the standee, she adds, "Tah-dah! We've made you kids brand ambassadors." And before any of us can comment, she rambles on, "This year's Valentine's Day campaign will be based on you two and your love story. We're launching a whole new line of chocolates, new boxes, and packaging all with your faces on it. You're going to be famous."

The standee is actually a display holder, from which Abigail retrieves a heart-shaped box. "I present you Bluewater Springs' newest raspberry and dark chocolate bonbon, the Chucokate."

Oh. My. Gosh.

They've combined our names as if we were a celebrity couple, and named the new product after us?

My heart sinks as Chuck's mom goes on. "And we've hired an Instagram expert to help make the campaign successful—Josiane Masson. She's a pretty big deal in the industry, and she'll be following you two around during the holidays. We've asked her to collect enough shots of you two turtle-doves to feed our social media accounts throughout February. And…" With a hand, she gestures at my dad. "Mick."

Dad smiles. "The projections for the Chucokate line are off the charts. All focus groups' polls came back enthusiastic. This rebranding will finally allow us to become a major player in the adult chocolate market."

A general round of applause greets this declaration. I can barely keep upright and fake-smiling. Chuck is as speechless as I am.

When the excitement marginally dies over, my mom turns to me. “But, Honeybun, what was it you wanted to tell us?”

I glance at the standee, trying to gauge how much money they’ve already sunk into the new campaign and how much the company stands to lose if we publicly break up and ruin the Chucokate love story.

I don’t know. A lot, most likely. But my brain is too tired to draw estimates right now.

Okay, Chuck, you win this round. The breakup announcement can wait until tomorrow.

“Nothing, Mom,” I say. Sagging back in my chair, I point at the standee. “The Chucokate is excitement enough for one night.”

More than a few disappointed looks cross the table. They were really hoping for a wedding announcement, weren’t they? I suppose it’d make the Chucokate story that much sweeter.

Dad is the quickest to recover. “Oh, well.” He pops the champagne cork. “To the Chucokate, then!”

The name is such a monstrosity it makes me wish the floor would open and swallow me whole. On my right, Chuck’s expression mirrors the same despair. Hard as it might’ve been to confess we’ve broken up before, now the situation has gone nuclear. Why didn’t we come clean four months ago?

Oh, gosh, Marco is going to kill me. I’d sworn I’d tell my parents as soon as I got home. He’s been getting sick and tired of having to listen to my calls with them where we talk about this fictional life where I’m still happily living with Chuck.

I’m so screwed.

Three

Chuck

Dinner is a disaster. I almost wish Kate and I had invented another fake trip and had not come home for the holidays.

No matter that this past Thanksgiving was possibly the saddest weekend of my life. I was alone at my buddy Daniel's place, where I'm still crashing on the couch. Kate tossed me to the curb at the beginning of the school year, making it impossible for me to find a half-decent, affordable house in Ann Arbor. Thanks again, Kate.

Anyway, I spent Thanksgiving alone, as all my friends had gone home for the long weekend. I ate a solo, microwaved lunch, since I was too depressed to cook a proper meal. The rest of the day I spent alternatively stalking Marco's Instagram and my mom's. The first provided romantic shot after romantic shot of their romantic Canadian gateway. Kate's face was never in the pictures for obvious secrecy reasons, but anonymous body parts appeared here and there, or the odd photo from behind. The worst one—joined feet under the sheets—made me want to puke. Mom's photo documentary of the holiday wasn't stomach-churning, but watching my loved ones enjoy the best homemade meal and many good times still made me tragically homesick.

Hard to call what I would consider sadder. To have stalked my ex's new boyfriend or my mother on socials. I even sunk as low as creating a fake Instagram account to watch Marco's stories without him knowing it was me. Talk about hitting rock bottom.

But, dreary as Thanksgiving was, today is making a good

show at competing for Chuck's Worst Day Ever. In fact, I'm ready to call it a night. Dinner is over, and we've all moved into the Warrens' cathedral-ceilinged living room for the traditional eggnog nightcap. Only this year, it comes out of a bottle as we're drinking our very own Bluewater Springs Chocolate Company's Vanilla Eggnog.

We started testing bottled eggnog a year ago in a few local supermarkets. At first, I was skeptical about producing store-bought eggnog, but one sample taste changed my mind. Probably because Dad and Lillian used the same recipe they'd been making at home forever. And the market agreed with me. This holiday season, we're rolling out our eggnog nation-wide with plans to go international. We're also adding a nutmeg flavor variant.

Delicious as the eggnog tastes, the syrupy drink isn't enough to sweeten the bitter pill that my life has become. So, the moment Nana Fern dozes off on the Warrens' couch, I seize my chance, gently elbowing my dad.

"Dad, it's getting late. Shouldn't we drive Nana Fern home?"

Dad pats my knee. "You're probably right, son."

"Mind if I catch a ride with you?" I ask. "I'm tired of driving."

"Nonsense," Lillian, Kate's mom, interjects from her seat on the couch perpendicular to ours. "You're sleeping here, Love."

"Here, you mean…"

"In Kate's room, of course."

Out of my control, my voice raises to a squeal. "I can't sleep in Kate's room!"

Kate, who's chilling by the fire with her dad, only catches this last part and turns to stare daggers at me. "What did you just say?"

"*I* didn't say anything," I defend myself. "Your mom is insisting I spend the night."

Alarm instantly replaces the annoyance on her face. "Mom, you seriously can't expect us to sleep together in a twin bed."

"Of course not, Honeybun."

"Oh. Good."

"That's why we've refurbished your room!" Lillian smiles proudly. "Tell her, Mick."

Kate's dad makes jazz hands. "Surprise!"

Kate reacts with an I've-had-enough-surprises-for-one-night face, and, for once, I agree with her. "What have you done to my room?" she says flatly.

"Not much, Honeybun, don't worry," Lillian says. "We've only upgraded the bed and added some closet space. Nothing too serious. All your stuff is still there."

"Thank you, Lillian," I say. "But I was looking forward to my bed and my room. I have all my stuff there."

"But it's already decided," Lillian says. "Josiane Masson said she'd rather have you both under the same roof—apparently it's easier to coordinate for the photo shoots. She also wants to snap a few spontaneous shots of you acting naturally as you eat breakfast in the morning all sleepy-eyed and in love…"

"Mom!" Kate says, sounding as determined to send me home as I am to go. "Chuck hasn't seen his parents in months. I'm sure they'll want to have some time together in private. Don't you, Abigail?" She looks hopefully toward my mother.

Mom, who's busy leafing through the latest issue of the Bluewater Springs Digest, raises her head. "Sorry, Darling, what did you say?"

"I was trying to explain to my mom how you surely want to have Chuck at home for the holidays."

Puzzled, Mom looks at Lillian. "Isn't Chuck sleeping here? I thought it was decided. I haven't made his bed or cleaned his room."

"See?" Lillian smiles in victory. "Chuck is staying. It's settled."

"Mom," I plead. "Are you sure you don't want me to come home with you? I can make the bed and clean the room, it's no big deal."

"But why would you, Darling?" She calls everyone 'darling'. Mom gets up and kisses both my cheeks. "You belong with Kate. Plus, we spend more time here than at our house, anyway." She nudges my dad. "Bud, we should really get going. Nana Fern is well past her bedtime."

I try not to freak out as my get-away-from-Kate plan leaves without me. A few Kate-free, drama-free hours were the only thing that has kept me pushing through this lousy day. I was craving the loneliness of my old room, where I could've relaxed on my own turf and read a book in peace or shot up a video game. I sure could tear to pieces a few goblins right now. It'd be great for my nerves.

And, if I had any doubts, the look Kate shoots me across the room promises anything but relaxation. Heck, she's probably going to make me sleep on the floor.

***

She doesn't send me straight to the floor, but that doesn't make our sleeping situation any more comfortable.

Tension radiates off Kate as she manhandles the bed, throwing off the covers like they personally offended her.

Grabbing the pillows, she constructs an impenetrable wall down the middle of the bed. "That's your side. Stay there."

I shrug. One side of the bed is way better than the floor, so I'm not complaining.

"I know you're probably heartbroken there's no PlayStation here," she continues, "but I'm sure you can survive a few hours without one."

Yeah, okay, the thought of powering up my old console and blowing off some steam with a game crossed my mind, but… "You know I'm not addicted to gaming?" I say. "I can live without my PlayStation."

Kate scoffs. "Yeah, right. Go tell that to someone who hasn't lived with you for the past three years."

Before I can reply, her phone starts to vibrate. She glares at me, pressing a finger to her mouth. "Not a word."

I drop on the bed and cross my arms over my chest while Kate moves closer to the window and picks up. "Hi, Marco."

I can't hear the other side of the conversation, but from Kate's answers, I'm pretty sure I know what they're discussing.

"Yes, it went well," she says. "No, no, they were a little shocked at first, but now they're happy for me… Yes, they can't wait to meet you… When? Uh? Spring break, maybe… No, it isn't worth making the trek up here sooner… Don't worry, I'm fine… Yeah… Me, too… Night."

I'm not sure what that "me, too" at the end stood for. Was it in response to *I miss you, me too?* Or a more serious *I love you, me too?* Could Kate really be in love with Sweaty Posts?

"That sounded an awful lot like you were lying," I say.

"I wasn't lying," Kate hisses as she sits on her side of the bed and gets under the covers. Despite the denial, her cheeks flush in that adorable way that used to make me lose my head. Still does. And is probably not the best thought to have before sharing a bed with my ex—pillow barrier or not.

"I was only anticipating the truth," Kate continues. "It doesn't matter if we tell our families tonight or tomorrow, the endgame won't change." She turns away from me and switches off the lights. "And now I would like to sleep, if you don't mind."

I don't even try to say I'd like to read awhile to avoid another pointless confrontation. I just lay there staring at the dark ceiling, wallowing in my misery. Morning will come soon. I can do this…

Four

Kate

Snuggled in comfy warmth, I inhale deeply, relishing in the knowledge I don't have to get up just yet. Also, for the first time in a long while, I feel at home.

Well, duh, you silly... because you're home.

For the holidays...

To tell my parents Chuck and I broke up...

The Chucokate!

I blink, suddenly wide-awake and in a state of panic.

Then I realize who I'm snuggling with and my mental health further deteriorates. I'm curled up against Chuck, my face resting on his chest and his stupid Star Wars pajamas, my feet comfortably nestled between his calves for warmth.

How did I end up sprawled on top of him?

I pull back, careful not to wake him, and assess the situation in the feeble light of pre-dawn.

We're on his side of the bed, so he didn't creep on me during the night. I must've rolled on top of him in my sleep. The floor is strewn with discarded pillows. I must've kicked them off the bed to clear my path to Chuck.

Well, it's not my fault. I've always been a hugger, and my subconscious perhaps still hasn't flagged Chuck as the enemy. Okay, maybe not an enemy, but an ex. Who I hope, one day, I'll be able to go back to being friends with. We just have to wait for all the hard feelings of the breakup to settle.

I look at him now, sleeping peacefully while the Darth Vader black mask on his chest moves up and down in rhythm with his breathing. He couldn't be nerdier if he tried, with his pale, I-spend-too-much-time-indoors-in-front-of-a-laptop skin and spaghetti-straight blue-black hair sticking out in all directions.

But he used to be *my* nerd. My blue-eyed, long-lashed, chiseled nerd.

An inexplicable lump rises in my throat.

How did I go from loving this man with everything I had, to barely being able to spend two minutes with him without arguing? A pang of regret beats against my chest from within.

Well, of course, Chuck is my first love. My first everything. I can't expect to get over him in just a few months after a decade as a couple and a lifetime as best friends.

But I must stay strong.

Remember the apathy, Kate, and everything else you came second to. The lack of initiative. The laziness. Our lives were diverging into opposite tangents. I simply called the end first.

Still, being home with him has not been the piece of cake I'd expected. Lots of buried feelings resurfacing, and our parents…

Oh, gosh. I hide my face in my hands as I envision the Chucokate standee again. Of all years, why did they have to pick this one to make us brand ambassadors?

The Valentine's Day campaign must be part of their not-so-secret plan to convince their only children to move back home once school is over and come work for The Bluewater Springs Chocolate Factory.

Another can of worms I don't care to open just now. I'm not clear what I want to do once I finish my MBA next summer, but I'm positive I could do without the pressure. I want to be free to decide on my own, without the guilty impression I'm letting someone down if I don't choose the path they've laid out for me.

Too many thoughts are jamming my brain. I get up and change into my thermal athletic gear, getting ready for a quick jog. I've wanted to get more fit forever, and Marco gave me the final push I needed to pick up running. He's full of life, full of interests, and exactly the kind of man I need by my side.

Careful to creak the bedroom door open as stealthily as I can, I'm about to slip out when I see Chuck lying on the bed half uncovered. He's going to catch a cold like that. I tiptoe to his side of the bed and pull the comforter up to his neck. I almost go for a kiss on the forehead but keep myself in check. Until we've adjusted to our exes status, we need to keep clear boundaries.

I walk away from the bed, out of the bedroom, and hop down the stairs—mindful to avoid the third-to-last step which always squeaks. At the front door, I zipper-up my running jacket and walk out onto the porch. I breathe in the cold air like a tonic and jog along the driveway, heading for the lake.

The sun is slowly rising as I cross the Bluewater Bridge, its rays igniting sparks in a million ice crystals dangling from every surface: tree branches, house roofs, streetlights. Every single house in town is decorated with Christmas lights. Many have an outdoor Christmas tree as well as an indoor one, and I pass countless snowmen along the way. From the simplest one to the most elaborate snow sculptures. Easy to guess which families will compete in The Bluewater Springs' Annual Snow Sculpting Challenge—sponsored, of course, by The Bluewater Springs Chocolate Company.

As I reach the town's square, the scenery becomes even more picturesque, resembling a holiday postcard. Weathered stone buildings with snowy rooftops encircle tall, ancient trees wrapped in fairy lights. The old-fashioned streetlamps are decorated with bows and garlands. And the quaint, glowing storefronts patiently await a new day of Holiday shopping.

In the heart of Old Town Square, a giant Christmas tree towers over the scene, complete with a life-size illuminated sleigh in front of it being pulled by no less than eight sparkly reindeer. In front of the sleigh, a red and white sign reads: Brought to you by The Bluewater Springs Chocolate Company.

I stare across the street at The Bluewater Springs Chocolate Company café, candy shop, gift shop, the boutique, and the Chocolate Factory Museum—all owned by my and Chuck's families.

The square is almost deserted at this hour with most of the shops still closed. But, as if on cue, the café lights switch to life and I head in that direction, ready for a white vanilla mocha, my favorite coffee order. I don't have my wallet, but Chuck and I never pay in the shops owned by our families. And, sometimes, we have a hard time paying even in the shops our folks don't own. Being a Warren or a Rose in Bluewater Springs is like being royalty.

As I push the door open, I stamp the snow off my sneakers, smiling at the plastic Santa Claus mounted on the threshold. The bell Santa is holding in one hand promptly jingles, and Saint Nick lights up to welcome me with a jolly *ho, ho, ho.*

"Hey, Mildred," I greet the barista. Being a one hundred percent family-owned business, we Warrens pride ourselves on knowing our employees by name. At least, the ones in Bluewater Springs. Not a challenge, considering Chuck and I have grown up in the halls of the Chocolate Factory—at one point literally—among candies and toys and basically the love of two moms, two dads, and our extended workforce family. Chuck and I have also been interns at the company in various roles, from business to production, to retail, to wholesale, since the ninth grade. So we know our people well.

The factory and its workers are like a second family to us. And from the day we could talk, our parents have been grooming us to take over one day. The Bluewater Springs Chocolate Company is our destiny. But with the expansion of the firm and its play to go international, working in the family business won't necessarily translate to returning to Bluewater Springs—at least, not for me. Chuck's dream is to move back home at once after graduation next summer. He wants to settle down and design new toy and apparel lines and never go anywhere else. Admittedly, he has a talent for product development. All the plush toys he designed outsold the others tenfold. Put a pencil in his hands and he comes alive.

Me, I'm more of a numbers girl, like my dad. And with the UK plant grand opening scheduled for next year, I could join the financial team in London. What an adventure it would be. But when I suggested the possibility, Chuck of course wouldn't hear of it. To get him off his precious couch is the worse offense one could ever pull on him. I don't know how he stays so fit, considering he never works out and eats like an unsupervised teenager whose been left in charge of doing the groceries. Chuck's not brawny, but he has defined, flat muscles, and a six-pack he honestly doesn't deserve.

He's one of those insufferable people who could eat a whole turkey and not gain a pound. Not fair. Especially when I have to be careful given the business our families are in.

The temptation to taste-test every new sweet we produce constantly lingers, but I have to keep track of every calorie if I don't want to gain ten pounds every time I come home. That's one of the things I intend to change as soon as I'm given more responsibility within the company. For years, I've been advocating for a reduction in our products' sugar levels and the necessity to bring to market lower-calorie, healthier alternatives. Mom has been skeptical, but she's agreed to give agave syrup a try in a few limited runs of our most basic sweets.

Baby steps.

"Kate," the young barista behind the counter welcomes me. "You and Chuck are back home?"

That's the other thing with Bluewater Springs. Since Chuck and I got together, I've ceased being a single entity and become merely one half of our duet. Ninety percent of the time people refer to me in the plural.

"Yeah," I say, "just last night."

"What are you doing out this early?"

"I took up running a few months ago."

"Oh, that's new." The barista smiles. "If I could've stayed warm in bed under the covers this morning, I surely would have. Especially if Chuck was there next to me."

Mildred's comment is meant to be a joke, but I can't help the wince that comes naturally to my lips. Chuck is by far the best catch in town, not only because our families are well off, but also because he's the hottest, kindest, sweetest guy in Bluewater Springs. Maybe all he needs is to meet a girl who's happy to live her entire life in this small town, and who enjoys watching *Star Trek* movies, playing video games, and who doesn't find cosplay ridiculous. Because Chuck is the personification of the hot nerd: shy and irresistible. And more than a few hearts broke in our community when the news got out that we were an item.

Well, ladies, he's going to be all yours again soon.

An image of Chuck running across the Bluewater Bridge chased by a horde of women in bridal wear crosses my mind. It might not happen exactly like that, but the moment Chuck moves home single, the town's bachelorettes will engage in a battle to the last blood to snatch him up. The thought makes me want to puke.

"Sorry, Kate," Mildred says. "I was joking. We all know Chuck only has eyes for you."

The affirmation depresses me even further and causes my stomach to swirl with guilt. From what I've heard—or, more accurately, *not* heard—from our shared friends back in Ann Arbor, Chuck hasn't been with anyone else since we broke up. Or, maybe, he's only been more discreet than me and has been having one torrid affair after the other.

Heat rushes to my cheeks. Let's not go there.

"No, Mildred, sorry. I have this awful cramp in my left calf." Plausible enough, as excuses come. "It gives me a bad case of resting bitch face every time. I wasn't upset with you."

"Oh, okay." Mildred huffs, relieved. No one wants to mess with the big boss's daughter.

Another aspect of Smallsville living that makes me look forward to the anonymity of London, where nobody will know who I am, or what my family does, or which man I was destined to marry from the womb. Our mothers even got pregnant within two weeks of each other.

"Should I get the usual started for you?" Mildred asks. "Vanilla white mocha?"

"Yes, please."

"Anything to eat?"

"No, thanks."

Mom will surely fix a massive breakfast at home and I don't want to spoil my appetite.

Five minutes later, Mildred hands me my drink. "Here you go, Kate, with an extra vanilla pump just like you like it."

I take the warm paper cup from her. "Thanks."

"By the way, are you excited about the new campaign?"

"Uh?"

"Oh my gosh, don't tell me I've spoiled the surprise. Mr. Warren and Mrs. Rose presented it at the company's Christmas party last week; they said they would tell you once you got home, and I just assumed—"

"Are you talking about the Chucokate?" I interrupt.

"Thank goodness you know already. Phew, for a moment I thought I'd dropped the ball."

"No, no, it's all right, they told us last night." I take a sip of coffee, relishing the wave of heat it brings to my system. "What—what did *you* think of the new chocolate?"

"Oh, it's delicious. The crunchy raspberries are a stroke of genius."

"I wasn't talking about the taste. What about the name? Don't you think it's a bit… uh… I don't know, over the top?"

"No." She actually bats her lashes dreamily. "It's so cute. You and Chuck are the perfect couple, so inspirational. You guys are going to become the next Brangelina."

I refrain from commenting that Brangelina is no more.

"You're lucky to have Chuck," Mildred continues.

"Every girl in town wishes she were you."

Yeah, right. I don't think so.

But I have to concede a point to Chuck's mom. The Chucokate might not be such a crazy idea. Pity it will never see the light of day.

The same sense of nausea that hits me whenever I imagine telling my parents the truth about Chuck and me promptly sucker-punches me in the stomach. I squash it with a sip of heavily-chocolated coffee.

I can't go on like this. We need to tell them soon, today, this morning. Otherwise, I'm going to develop a stress ulcer.

Once I'm properly warmed and caffeinated, I prepare for the run back home, re-tying my laces and pulling up a new playlist on my phone.

I've just walked out of the café when my phone rings. It's Marco.

"Hey," I pick up, my breath pluming in the frosty air.

"Hey, babe, I missed you on my run this morning."

"Yeah, me, too."

"You done already?"

"Actually, no, I was heading back home now. I had a bit of a late start," I say. Because for Marco, seven a.m. is late. He's really into fitness and keeping a balanced diet and a healthy lifestyle.

"Read me your stats so far?"

Marco made me download a fitness app to track my progress. I open it now on my phone while hopping from foot to foot to keep warm. The numbers aren't awful, but I still round them up a bit. I give myself an extra mile and shave a few minutes off the total running time. Only because Marco is fixated on constant improvement. Maybe a little too fixated.

"That's great, babe! Keep going like this and you'll be able to run the Point-to-point half-marathon in June."

"Uh, I'm not sure about that. I could enroll in the 10k version like we talked about."

"Don't sell yourself short, babe. If you train hard enough, you'll make it."

Sometimes Marco can be a bit condescending, and maybe a little irritating, too. Because, yes, I know I can complete a thirteen-mile race if I set my mind to it. But the idea just doesn't appeal to me. I don't care about marathons or half-marathons. For me, running isn't about the competition, not even with myself—it's just a fun, healthy exercising habit.

But, hey, *I* wanted to be with someone who encouraged me to become a better version of myself and pushed me to achieve more. Yeah, I should remember that. Marco is good for me. I like how energetic, vital—

"Provided you don't eat too much sugar during the holidays."

I throw a guilty stare at the café behind me. Marco takes his coffee black. No sugar, no milk, no chocolate, and definitely not a double shot of vanilla syrup.

Whatever. It's Christmas. A small cup won't kill me. "I'll do my best," I say. "But you know sugar kind of *is* the family business."

"I'm only reminding you not to overindulge. If you go off on a tangent even for just a couple of weeks it could take months to get back in shape."

"Yeah, yeah, sure. Listen, I'm kind of freezing my ass off. Mind if we talk later?"

"Oh, you're not running? I thought you said you were only halfway done?"

"Yeah," I confirm, annoyed. "But I've stopped to talk to

you. I can't run and talk at the same time. I don't have the stamina for that yet."

"You need to work on your breathing, babe. Where there's a will, there's a way."

"Well, yeah, I'll work my way up to it. But now I really have to go. Talk later?"

"Later, babe."

We hang up, and I blast *Tones and I* by Dance Monkey at top volume on my phone to run back home.

Marco is right about one thing, though: where there's a will, there's a way. I can apply the same principle to confessing the truth to my parents. It's only a matter of taking a deep breath and making the plunge. As soon as I get home, I'm going to kick Chuck off the bed—he'll surely be still asleep—and drag him downstairs to come clean with our parents if it's the last thing I do.

Five

Chuck

I wake up with the smell of Kate's hair filling my nostrils. For a moment I think I'm dreaming, until I look down and find my ex spread-eagled over me.

Did I trespass over the pillows and grab her in the middle of the night? I check the bed, but I'm still squarely on my half of the mattress. Kate is the intruder. She's resting her cheek on my chest while her feet are nestled between my calves in the same position we always sleep in—or at least, used to.

I don't know what to do. What I *want* to do is hold her tight and never let her go. What I *should* do, however, is roll her to her half of the bed before she wakes up and freaks out.

I compromise by doing nothing, simply enjoying this moment of rare peace between us. She's the one on top of me, after all. It's not my job to move.

Kate stirs in her sleep, sending me into a panic. What now?

I shut my eyes and do my best to play dead.

Kate inhales deeply, then raises her head slightly while I pretend to still be asleep. I can picture the small frown of confusion on her face as she takes in the new sleeping arrangements. I half expect her to shoot to her side of the bed, appalled, but she doesn't. She remains curled against me for a heartbeat longer before she slowly retreats, leaving me cold and exposed. A metaphor of the past few months.

Her weight is still on the mattress, but she isn't lying down. I imagine her sitting against the headboard with her knees tucked under her chin, thinking.

What are you thinking, Kate?

I'd pay millions to know.

A few more minutes, and she moves again and gets up. Rustling noises ensue, and I listen as she gets dressed.

A zipping sound signals she's done. Muffled steps approach the bed and Kate gently tucks me under the covers she'd lowered getting up. Such a simple gesture, but one so tender it makes my brain short-circuit with unanswered questions.

Then the bedroom door clicks shut, and Kate's gone.

Two minutes later, the front door opens and shuts as well. I hurry to the window to spy on my ex. Where is she going this early in the bone-chilling Michigan cold?

Kate jogs along the driveway, leaving small footprints on the thin layer of snow that fell during the night. Her clothes look super professional. Since when is she into running?

There's so much already I don't know about her and this new life she's created for herself. This new life she doesn't want me to be a part of.

Unable to go back to sleep, I take a shower and change into jeans and my favorite Chocolate Company sweater. In fact, I designed this one. The concept isn't revolutionary or anything, but I love the dark green color and the comical red-nosed reindeer.

By the time I get downstairs, Lillian is already making breakfast. I help her set the kitchen table, my mind already whirring through possible escape strategies. I need to leave before Kate gets back, that much is obvious. I want to spend a few quiet hours by myself in my room without any disappointed looks or breakup talk.

I fill a mug with coffee and grab a cinnamon roll that I

devour in four quick bites as Lillian would never let me leave on an empty stomach.

"Lillian, your rolls are the most delicious," I say.

"Thank you, Love. You want another one?"

"Uh? No, thanks. Actually, I was thinking of dropping by my parents' house to grab a few things. I wasn't expecting to be staying with you… So, well, I'm gonna get going, okay?"

"Oh, are you sure? What are you missing? Maybe we have extra in the house."

"Err, no, just stuff… I'd really rather go home."

"Okay, but remember to be back by ten-thirty."

"Why?"

"Josiane Masson is coming to meet you and Kate?"

"Who?"

"Josiane Masson—the Instagram guru your mom hired to promote the Chucokate. Remember?"

"Ah, yeah, sure."

I definitely didn't remember we were meeting her today. Bummer.

Lillian stops stirring the pancake mix and eyes me suspiciously. "Are you okay, Love?"

"No. I mean, yeah, totally." I'm the worst liar in the world. I'd better get out of here fast. "I'll be back in time to meet Josiane Masson."

"Here." Lillian cleans her hands on her apron and offers me a plate of her famous double chocolate chip cookies. "At least take a cookie for the road."

I grab one and hug her goodbye. In the hall, I hold the cookie between my teeth as I pull on my coat and leave the house. As the first gust of chilly morning air hits my face, I take a bite, and mmm… the chocolate melts in my mouth. By the time I've crossed the front yard to reach the rental car,

I've eaten every last crumb.

I get into the car, grab the wheel, and my hands nearly become frost-glued to the plastic. I blow hot air on my fingers and pull out the gloves from my coat pockets. The Nissan's engine takes a minute to tremble to life and, after blasting the heating at tropical temperatures, I reverse the rented compact. The tires skid on the ice, but I manage to reel them under control and head down the driveway—only to slam on the brakes as I spot Kate running toward me from the opposite direction.

Her eyebrows draw together and, in a few, quick strides she's level with the car.

Resigned to my fate, I roll down the window.

"Morning," I say.

She attacks right away. "Where do think you're going?"

"Home."

"Why?"

"I need some quiet, Kate. I don't want to be stuck at your house with you and your parents, playing the happy couple all morning."

"Good, neither do I. We have to tell them the truth. Now."

That's the last thing I want to do at the moment. "Don't you want to take a shower first? And your dad isn't even up yet. There's no rush."

"I can take a quick shower, and I'm sure Dad will be up before I'm finished." She sets her jaw stubbornly. "We're doing this, Chuck. Get on board."

"And what about *my* parents? Mom and Dad would hate to be the second ones to learn the truth."

"We can go tell them right afterward, I'm sure half an hour won't make much of a difference."

I never thought I'd say this, but thank goodness for

Josiane Masson. "There isn't enough time," I inform Kate.

Her eyes narrow. "Why not?"

"That Instagram lady is coming over at ten-thirty to meet us."

"No. No. No. We have to stop this madness before it goes any further. We can't let them believe we're going along with the Chucokate." She pauses. "Maybe you were right."

Me, right? This must be a first.

"About what?" I ask.

"I should tell my parents, and you yours. And we can all reassemble here afterward at ten-thirty and inform the Instagram lady her services won't be needed after all. We'll also have to brainstorm a new name for the Chucokate. It'll make for an awkward holiday, but we always knew it would. It's time to end this."

Well, there's no changing her mind when she gets like this. Dread fills me, but also a weird sense of anticipation. I can't wait to drop this weight off my chest. To be free. And to quit all the lies.

I grip the wheel and stare at Kate. "Okay," I say. "We tell them now. No excuses."

Her features set in a determined expression, and she nods. "Now. No excuses."

Kate takes a step back away from the car, and I return the nod as I raise the window.

Truth, here I come.

***

I arrive at home filled with good intentions. I mean to march in there, call a family gathering, and set things straight. But nothing ever goes according to plan, and the road to hell is famously paved with good intentions.

Mine shatter when I run into Nana Fern in the hall the moment I step into the house. She grabs my elbow and asks me to follow her into her studio. Nana Fern used to be an artist, like me—a painter.

She doesn't paint anymore—her eyesight is too poor now—but the art studio is still her favorite room in the house. The space is awash in light, which streams in from the wall-wide windows at the back.

The view of the backyard is always stunning, but in winter, the garden is straight out of a fairytale. Open grounds extend out of sight in a wintry wonderland. Every tree, bush, and surface is coated in puffy snow that glitters in the sun.

Nana Fern spends most of her time in this room. She used to either paint on her easel or sit in the sunshine and read, but nowadays she'll just relax and listen to audiobooks. I shop for her remotely or whenever I'm home, and I've taught her how to talk to her phone to load them up. I've also installed a Wi-Fi speaker system in the studio so the sound is top quality. And Nana has mastered voice control.

She guides me to the couch at the back of the room, the one nestled underneath the wide windows. We sit and contemplate the view for a few long seconds; it's impossible not to be momentarily awestruck.

Then Nana Fern sighs and tears her eyes away, taking my hands in hers.

Now I become worried. This is too much ceremony to simply have a "welcome home" conversation. "Nana Fern, is everything okay?"

"Yes, Dear, better than okay."

My shoulders relax; she's not about to tell me she's ill or anything. Well into her eighties, Nana Fern is old, but I'm not prepared to say goodbye to her. I'll never be.

"Chuck," she continues. "I'm so very proud of you, of everything you've accomplished with your life, and of the wonderful woman you have by your side."

Oh my gosh, please let this not be about Kate.

"It seems only yesterday that you were a little boy pestering me to read you one last bedtime story. But a boy, alas, you are no longer. You're a man now. Next year you'll be finished with grad school and you must think about the future. And you know what they say?"

"No, Nana."

"There are no great men without an exceptional woman by their side."

Ah, definitely about Kate. Just what I needed to relax: a little Kate-is-wonderful propaganda.

"Nana, I know you like Kate. But..."

"No buts, Dear. You're never going to find a better woman than her. You are destined to be together, and nothing would bring me more joy than to see the two of you settle down before I die."

Oh, come on, how is that fair? She can't play the death card! Low blow. How am I supposed to segue into my Kate-dumped-me news now? Nana Fern would probably have a stroke if I told her right after she made such a heart-felt declaration.

When in doubt, stall.

"Nana, we're still young. There's no rush."

"But why wait? You never know what life might throw at you. Look at me and your grandfather. He was taken away from me too young, and my sole consolation was that we'd gotten married as early as we could."

Cold sweat makes my hands clammy. Not only is Nana giving me a pep talk about proposing to my ex-girlfriend, but she's coming at me with the heavy guns. A double death card—about herself and grandpa—in the space of five minutes? What even brought all of this on?

I don't have to wait long to find out.

Nana lets go of my hands and takes a small red velvet box with gold trimming out of her pocket. The box would be the perfect size to carry a ring.

Oh.

Oh *no*.

This can't be happening.

"What's this?" I ask, strangled.

She gives me a kind smile. "Open it."

I take the box from her and pop the lid. Inside is a golden ring with a red stone mounted atop. It's clearly an antique, and the band is embossed with ornate swirls that speak of a bygone era. Kate would adore it.

I jerk the lid shut again and try to swallow, but I can't. My throat has clogged, and I'm having difficulty breathing.

"T-thanks, Nana," I force out. "But I don't think Kate and I are ready for marriage."

I try to give the box back, but Nana Fern closes my hand over it with hers. "Keep it, Dear. One day you'll be ready to propose to Kate, and I want you to do it with the same ring your grandfather gave me. The ring has been in our family for five generations." Then she sighs again. "Well, I hope I'll still be around when you finally decide to do it."

She pats my hand. Can this woman guilt-trip or what?

"I'll take the box, Nana, but don't expect any news soon."

"I've lived long enough to learn to never say never." Nana throws me a little wink. "Now, can you help me find this new book I've heard so much about…?"

"What book?"

Nana feeds me a few major plot points that I type into Google, and we're able to find the title. I load the audiobook then flee the studio, craving the solitude of my room.

The past twenty-four hours have felt like a relentless struggle between myself and the Universe. Me, trying to get to my room to be in peace for five minutes. The Universe, doing its best to prevent me.

And Mr. Cosmos isn't finished yet.

Down the hall, I run into my mom.

For a second, she's startled at finding me in the house. Then her gaze lowers to my hands and, for someone who wears glasses and has none on now, she spots the tiny red box I'm holding with disarming quickness.

"Oh my gosh, Chuck! You asked Nana Fern for her engagement ring."

"No, Mom," I say, raking a hand through my hair. The situation is getting out of control. "Nana Fern forced the family heirloom on me, saying I should propose to Kate."

"Well, are you? Will you?"

"No, Mom, Kate and I are nowhere near ready for marriage."

"But why not? You've been in love forever, you've known each other even longer, and besides, your father and I were young when—"

Before she can launch into another speech to remind me how young everyone in this family got married, or that at my age, she was already pregnant with me, and you and Kate don't want to be old parents and all that, I stop her. "I know, Mom, I know." I give her a quick hug and a kiss on the cheek. "But… different times. I'm going to my room now. I have to be back at Kate's in less than an hour."

"Oh, yes, to meet Josiane Masson. We're all going."

"Great, I'll be down in half an hour."

I shuffle past her and speed walk to my room.

Once inside, I shut the door behind me and drop on the bed. I hit my forehead with the red box repeatedly.

Hell, here I come.

Six

Kate

The crunching of tires on snow alerts me to Chuck's return. I hurry to the window in time to see the Roses' Grand Cherokee park next to my dad's Cadillac SUV. Chuck's mom gets out and, from the way Abigail is smiling and obviously in a good mood, it's clear Chuck has gone back on his word and hasn't told his parents a damn thing.

The Nissan pulls up behind Bud's Jeep soon afterward, and Chuck steps out. I race down the stairs, taking the steps two at a time, to intercept him, and throw the front door wide open before Abigail can ring the bell—not that she ever does, since they usually just walk in.

"Oh, hi, Darling," she says, surprised.

"Hi, I need to talk to Chuck."

"Bud, would you look at this," she says, addressing her husband. "One hour apart, and the kids can barely survive! It's so sweet." Then, turning back to me. "Chuck is all yours, Darling."

Abigail steps aside to let her son in.

I grab Chuck's hand and pull him across the threshold none-too-gently.

"Ow," Chuck protests.

"We'll be back in a second," I inform his parents with a sugary sweet smile.

"You'd better be," Bud says with a smile. "Josiane Masson will arrive soon, and we don't want to keep her waiting."

I drag a morose-looking Chuck up the stairs to my room

and, once we're behind closed doors, I wheel on him.

"You didn't tell them!" I accuse. "How could you not? You promised."

"Yeah, I know, but something big came up and—Wait, did *you* tell your parents?"

Nope. I chickened out. Not that he needs to know that. "No, but—"

"Then what gives you the right to yell at me?"

"I didn't speak with my parents only because I knew you'd go back on your word."

"I could say the same."

"When have I ever gone back on my word?"

"When have I?"

"Just now."

"You, too."

This argument is childish, pointless, and isn't leading us anywhere. Also, I'm more than a little disappointed in myself for crumbling under the pressure. When I got home, Mom was singing and dancing around the kitchen as she fixed breakfast, and I couldn't bring myself to dampen the mood. And when Dad came down to eat he just wouldn't shut up about all the plans he has for the Chucokate. It never seemed the right moment to shatter all their dreams and hopes.

"Wait," I say, frowning. "Something 'big' came up? I'm having a hard time believing it could be bigger than this Chucokate disaster."

With a glum expression, Chuck buries one hand in his jeans pocket, takes out a tiny red velvet box, and slams it into my hands. "This big enough for you? Nana Fern gave me this when I got home, alongside a grand speech about how the only thing that can possibly make her happy before she kicks the bucket is to see us get married."

I stare at the box. "Is this what I think it is?"

Chuck scoffs. "See for yourself."

I flip the lid and stare at the most beautiful antique ring I've ever seen. The elaborate gold band is exquisite, and the ruby set in the middle sparkles like a Christmas tree bulb.

A breath catches in my throat, and my heart cracks a little because, if Chuck and I were still together, and he had one day proposed to me, Nana's ring would've been the perfect engagement ring.

"This farce is getting out of hand," Chuck says, glaring down at the ring. "Nana Fern gives me a ring and flat out tells me to propose, and now my mom thinks I'm going to ask you to marry me any minute, and hasn't stopped smiling ever since—"

"Why? Why would your mom think you wanted to propose?"

"She saw me with the box and started building castles in the air no matter how many times I told her I don't want to propose."

Okay, for real this time. No more waiting. For either of us.

"Chuck, we can't keep going like this."

He sighs. "I know."

"Let's go downstairs and tell them, right now. Together, so we can't chicken out on our own. It's the right thing to do."

"Yeah, I agree."

As I start to close the box, the ruby on the ring glints invitingly. I'm struck by an irresistible urge to try the ring on, considering I'll probably never get the chance again. I try to remove it from its stand, but the band is wedged in tightly. I end up pulling too hard, and the ring flies out of my hands and tumbles under the bed.

"Hey, be careful." Chuck takes the box back from me and squats on the floor. "I get you don't want the ring, but no need to throw it away."

"Ha ha. Just find it. Need a light?"

"I think I'm good…"

He slithers under the bed with his bum sticking out in the air, then comes out again with the ring in one hand and the box in the other.

Chuck sits on his heels for a second and blows dust off the ring. Just when he's about to stand up, lifting on one knee, the door flies open. We both freeze. My mom is standing in the doorway and has already started talking. "Josiane has arrived, kids, she's waiting for you down—"

She stops mid-sentence as she takes in the scene. I follow her gaze to Chuck, who's currently on one knee with a ring in his hands, facing me. The shock on my mom's face quickly transforms into unadulterated joy as she jumps to all the wrong conclusions.

"It's happening!" she screeches. "Abigail, Mick, Bud… Chuck is proposing!"

"Mom, he's not—it's not…"

I don't know why I bother. She's so excited she's not taking in a word I'm saying.

In a surprisingly short amount of time for a group of middle-aged people who have to run up a steep staircase, the other parents arrive and crowd the threshold behind my mom. Abigail is already crying.

They stare at us, and we stare back. Chuck is still kneeling on the ground. I think he was too shocked to think of standing up. Understandable, considering I was too shocked to pull him to his feet myself.

"Come on, Honeybun," my mom urges. "Don't mind us. Give the poor boy an answer!"

"He hasn't asked any question," I point out, in a voice raspy with terror.

Chuck's gaze shifts from me to the parents, and then back. "Uh…"

"Ooh, then we haven't missed the big event!" his mom cheers.

"Come on, Chucky," Bud encourages him. "You can do it, my boy."

Chuck clears his throat. "Kate… err…"

Oh my gosh. What is he doing? He can't seriously ask me to marry him.

Chuck Rose, don't you dare!

Oblivious to my mental threats Chuck stutters, "Will you… uh… mmm…"

I glare at him and shake my head ever so slightly, my gaze promising a swift and painful death if one more word comes out of his mouth.

"Will you… marry me?"

He actually did it. He said the words.

I stare at him, flabbergasted, as our parents all burst into tears—even the dads. I honestly don't think I've ever seen them this happy, while all I want to do is to disapparate from the room.

With all eyes on me, I give the only possible answer. "Y-Yes?"

So much for ending the farce. Now we're off the deep end and into monster-infested waters. And my sole companion in this ocean of despair is a terrified-looking nerd who clearly has no more idea of what to do in this crazy situation than I do.

Chuck, looking as horrified as I feel, stands up and takes my hand. Both our hands are shaking with jitters and emotions opposite to those one should feel on such an occasion. Dread instead of excitement. Anger instead of love. Misery instead of joy.

All eyes are still on us as Chuck awkwardly slides the ring onto my finger. A storm rages in his beautiful blue eyes—confusion, desperation, dismay… and also some deeper, buried emotion I can't read.

As I stare down at my ring finger, my hand has never felt heavier. A weird sense of foreboding wraps tightly around my chest.

The parents couldn't be in a more different emotional state. They erupt in cheers and applauses. Sounds that mix with the clear noise of a phone camera snapping photos. Looking past my dad, I notice for the first time a short brunette with a tight bun and winter-chic clothes—cream wool poncho, whitewashed jeans, and beige suede boots—staring back at me.

The woman snaps one last shot and then turns to Chuck's mom. "Oh, they're just perfect," Josiane Masson enthuses. "The engagement is going to do wonders for the Chucokate campaign."

So much for 'if there's a will, there's a way'. Will has nothing to do with it. It's clear to me now that the only law determining my fate is Murphy's Law: Anything that *can* go wrong *will* go wrong.

Seven
Chuck

The morning passes in a blur of mothers fawning over us, dads smoking cigars as they anticipate a new Warren-Rose generation, and a perfect stranger directing Kate and me into what feels like a million engagement photos. But the tears of joy in Nana Fern's eyes are the hardest to bear.

"Oh, Dear, you had me scared this morning with all your 'I'm not ready' and 'These are different times' talk. But I knew you only needed a little push. You've made me the happiest grandma on the planet."

The pressure is tightening around me like a boa constrictor. How is it that, every time we try to stop lying, we just dig ourselves deeper? Assuming we don't tell them over Christmas, and go along with the whole Chucokate madness until February… Then what? We can't just continue to pretend we're together for the rest of our lives.

I have no idea what Kate is thinking, as we haven't been alone for a second since the accidental proposal. And I'm a little ashamed to confess I'm glad a private conversation will have to wait until tonight after dinner. This afternoon, I have to go Christmas shopping—and, yeah, Kate had a point, I shouldn't have left it to the last minute, I certainly don't need the additional stress. Then I have to meet a few of my buddies for a beer. Meanwhile, Kate has been conscripted by the moms. The official reason is to spend a "girls only" afternoon, but I suspect they want to talk shop and get started on the wedding planning. Poor Kate, I sure don't envy her.

***

As expected, my last-minute Christmas shopping blitz is incredibly draining. After many years of giving original gifts to my beloved ones, coming up with fresh ideas has become hard. I miss being a little boy, when one of my drawings would do the trick. Or the easy first Christmases when it was wool hats, gloves, and a scarf for everybody. This year, it takes all my creativity to pick items people don't own already. Or, at least, I hope they don't.

For Mom, a temperature control smart mug because she constantly complains about her coffee getting cold before she finishes it. Dad's gift is not original, but always appreciated: every December I check his stock of spices at home and replenish it. Lillian, a new set of pot holders and an oven glove—today at breakfast I noticed her current ones are pretty worn out. Mick has been obsessing about the future of bees lately, so when I see the local gourmet store offers a program to adopt a beehive long-distance and receive the honey once a year, I sign him up and get a certificate to give to him on Christmas Day. Nana Fern is the easiest to sort with an audiobook subscription. Pops Teddy, a weighted gravity blanket—supposedly the best accessory for a profound rest. And then there's Kate.

What do I get my ex-girlfriend slash fake-fiancée, knowing that she'll open the present in full view of our entire family? It has to be something thoughtful and personal, but not so thoughtful and personal that Kate thinks I'm still in love with her.

I finally settle on one of those health & fitness smartwatches with a built-in GPS. Sure, she'll probably use it with Marco. If his Instagram account is any indication, I bet he's behind the sudden early morning fitness madness.

Still, Kate will like the smartwatch, so, what the heck, why not?

I load all the shopping bags in the trunk of the rental car and then set out for the pub, more than ready to spend a few hours catching up with my friends.

The Plough and Harrow is one of the oldest buildings in town. It dates back to the late 1800s, and it still has the original placard and woodwork. The interior is mostly authentic as well; only the emerald green and gold carpet panels on the walls and booth upholstery have changed over the generations of pub-owners. The counter, tables, floor, and ceiling are made of dark wood that's older than anyone inside.

An equally old iron chandelier dominates the center of the room, and antique light fixtures hang from the walls. They provide little illumination, but the semi-darkness is part of the charm of The Plough and Harrow. Also, there aren't any TV screens behind the bar or mounted on the walls. Stanley, the owner, has stubbornly refused to put one up forever. *"This is a place where people come to socialize,"* he'd say. *"My pub is a family environment. Good for storytelling, singing, and laughter. Not to get brainwashed in front of a TV. If you want that, go to The Red Wings,"* he would add with disdain, referring to the new sports bar near Route 31.

And, to be honest, Stanley has a point. As I walk in, the atmosphere couldn't be more relaxed, cheerful, and welcoming. Groups of people are gathered around chatting happily and guffawing. The holiday decorations draped on every surface and hook make the place even more holly-jolly.

I close the door behind me and take off my hat and gloves as a draft of warm air engulfs me. I ruffle up my flattened hair and spot Finn, Gary, and Phil seated at a high table. Gary catches my eye and waves. I trudge through the crowded room to reach them and sigh in relief at the four beers resting on the table. Great, the line at the bar is huge.

I sit on a high stool and finish removing my scarf and jacket before clasping hands with each of my friends.

The last time we met in person was at the end of summer, and I've missed them. Also, since I couldn't be honest about the Kate situation, I haven't kept in touch as much as usual. Phil works in New York, Gary is in med school at Stanford, and Finn is doing his master's at the University of Arizona. All places far away enough from Ann Arbor they wouldn't find out the truth by chance.

They promptly hassle me about the disappearing act. But, once the bantering is over and the first beer is gone, I can't help but notice Finn seems to be making an effort to appear happy while coming off even more tortured than I am.

"Hey, man, is everything all right? What's up with you?"

Phil answers for him. "Eva broke up with him."

"No," I say. "When?"

"Just before the holidays, dude, it sucks."

"Why?"

"She said she felt claustrophobic in our relationship and that it'd gotten too serious too fast."

"Sorry, man," I say, unable to express how much genuine sympathy I feel for him.

"Yeah," Finn says, and takes a long sip of beer. "You're lucky you've got Kate."

At this affirmation, Gary and Phil exchange a look.

"What?" I ask.

"Although," Gary says. "We heard some rumors…"

"What rumors?" I ask, instantly on guard.

"Well, Stella told Bea's sister who told me…"

I struggle to wrap my head around the gossip flow. Bea is Gary's girlfriend, who has a younger sister, Mia, but I don't know who this Stella person is. "Who's Stella?"

"Thomas MacArthur's younger sister," Phil says, naming one of our classmates from high school. "She's Mia's best friend."

"Okay," I say, making a go-on gesture at Gary.

"She goes to Kenyon College, but was at Ann Arbor for Halloween, and she swore she saw Kate kissing another guy. She couldn't be one hundred percent sure because the dude was wearing a Batman costume, but she said he was too ripped to be you. But Kate only had cat ears on and Stella recognized her."

The new info that Kate and Marco dressed as Batman and Catwoman for Halloween punches me in the gut harder than it should. Maybe because I'm such a nerd, but Kate knows *Batman Returns* is my all-time favorite Batman movie. And I know they've done worse than stealing my childhood heroes, like having sex—gag—but this is a low blow. It feels scornful and personal.

Thankful for the low lighting that hopefully won't allow the others to notice how red my neck and ears have turned, I try to laugh it off. "Come on, guys, of course it was me. I mean, Michael Keaton, Michelle Pfeiffer, directed by Tim Burton. If that doesn't have Chuck Rose written all over it, I don't know what does. And I used one of those foam body-suits that beef you up and make you seem all muscles."

Gary and Phil exchange another look. I'm not sure why, but they're not buying into my very credible explanations.

Gary says, "Well, Stella also said she spotted Kate the next morning with a dude of the same build. They were jogging together."

"Yeah, so what?"

"She hinted they looked pretty cozy with each other."

Ugh. Damn Stella. I don't even know her and she's ruining my life. "Guys, that's Marco," I say. The best lies are always sprinkled with truth. "They're running partners, nothing more."

The last thing Kate and I need is for a rumor that she's cheating on me to spread. Small town gossip can be deadlier than a shark with the scent of blood in its nostrils—which is how I picture the worst gossipers, anyway.

"Are you sure nothing shady is going on, man?" Finn asks. "I thought everything was good with Eva until she gave me the *hasta la vista* speech."

"No, yeah, plus Marco has a girlfriend. Amanda, Amelia, Angelina… something that starts with A…"

"Really? And him having a girlfriend is enough to sleep well at night? They could both be cheating on—"

"Listen, guys," I interrupt. "Kate and I are fine."

I'm beginning to sound desperate, and I can see it reflected in the skeptical stares of my friends, which makes me panic even more. So, before I've had time to reflect on the soundness of what I'm about to do, I blurt out, "In fact, we're more than okay. We're engaged."

"What?" Phil shouts.

"Seriously, man? Why didn't you tell us right away?" Finn asks.

"Guess I haven't really processed it myself yet. It just happened." Now that I've made the announcement, I try to downplay it. "Like, literally only a few hours ago."

"Man, you're talking as if you were surprised yourself," Gary points out.

I scratch the back of my head. "I kinda am, man. It wasn't planned, you know." At least this part is true. "But then this morning Nana Fern gave me the ring… and the proposal sort of followed naturally." More like *tragically*, and totally by accident.

Finn hollers his approval while Gary slaps me on the shoulder and Phil shakes my hand. "Cool, man, congratulations!" Finn says. "We must celebrate."

Gary stands up. I try to stop him, saying the engagement is not official yet, but he's already halfway to the bar and waves me off to go order another round of beers. I can't hear what my friend is telling Stanley, the pub owner, but from the way the barman's head snaps in my direction, he must've told him about the engagement. And the few patrons near Gary probably heard as well, because their heads turn my way, too.

Helplessly, I watch as the news spreads across the pub faster than a wildfire, in a wave of turning heads and whispered gossip.

The broadcast, however, doesn't stop within these walls. Soon, people are bringing out their phones and texting relatives, friends, and everyone else who might be bothered to know.

I shouldn't be surprised. A wedding between the two heirs to the chocolate crown is big news in Bluewater Springs.

And I'm a dead man.

The only chance Kate and I had to contain this morning's disaster was for no one to find out. And I just blew that possibility.

I'm so dead.

So. Dead.

Eight
Kate

I'm in hell.

The next time I see Chuck I'm going to kill him. That would solve all my problems: no fake fiancé, no fake engagement, no fake wedding to plan.

This has positively been the most miserable afternoon of my life. I'm drowning in wedding talk and surrounded by overexcited women: Mom, Abigail, Nana Fern, Aunt Muriel, my cousin Gretchen, and Josiane Masson—who seems committed to documenting every single moment of our fake relationship on camera for the world to see. The men—Pops and the dads—have been banished to the refurbished barn, lucky them. And I've no idea where Chuck has snuck off to, leaving me to hang.

I've been cornered and held captive in the living room since after lunch, being forced to listen to these smothering, nuptials-craving women ramble about wedding plans for hours. I've had to fend off one useless question after the other about a wedding that will never happen: summer or winter? Big or small? What color scheme? Where do we want to do it? And on and on…

Never mind how many times I tried to pass the message that just because Chuck and I got engaged today, it doesn't mean the wedding will be soon—or ever. No matter what I said, they point-blank ignored all my objections. Of course, I didn't disclose the one piece of the puzzle that could shut them up for good: that Chuck and I are no longer together, and the engagement is merely a huge misunderstanding. But

I put forward plenty of plausible explanations for why we'd want to wait. We're still young, we have to finish school first, maybe travel the world before we settle down…

Nothing. My words kept going into one ear and out the other, leaving no impressions on the brains in between.

Mom and Abigail have been so determined to see their two only children married to each other that, now that the dream is finally within their reach, they can't feign even the smallest amount of self-control. They're acting like over-sugared toddlers.

"What about the dress?" Aunt Muriel asks. "Do you know what shape you're going for? With your figure, you'd look stunning in a mermaid dress."

"But," Abigail cuts in, "wouldn't a princess gown with a wide skirt be more of a statement, like in a fairytale?"

"Ball gowns convert very well on socials," Josiane Masson says. "They receive an average of twenty percent more likes."

Nana Fern sighs. "The simpler, the more elegant, Dear. None of those crystal appliqués I see so often on the TV."

Mom cuts into the conversation. "Stop the nonsense, gals." I stare up at her with a glimmer of hope. Has someone finally realized how ludicrous the debate about a non-existent dress for a non-existent wedding has become? But then Mom finishes the phrase: "Kate is going to wear my wedding dress. It's tradition."

A general intake of breath seizes the room, and all eyes turn on me. I do my best not to cringe. My parents got married ages ago and Mom's dress is close in style to Princess Diana's wedding gown, which might've been all the rage after the royal wedding but definitely isn't my style.

I smile with a non-committal, "We'll see."

Mom goes all teary-eyed. "Actually, would you… would you want to try it on?"

An even louder collective gasp spreads among the crowd.

The darkening sky provides me with the perfect excuse. "What if Chuck comes back and sees me, Mom? It'd be such bad luck."

"Oh, don't worry, Darling," Abigail says. "Chuck is having a beer at The Plough and Harrow with Gary, Phil, and Finn. He texted me earlier. I don't expect him to come home before dinner."

Is there smoke coming out of my ears and nostrils? There must be, because I'm fuming. Chuck is out having the time of his life with friends, while I have to sit here and endure *this!*

"Wonderful," Mom says. "I'll go fetch the dress from the attic."

The loft is directly above the living room, which my parents kept at double the height of all the other rooms in the house without a second story. From down here, we can hear her scrape around and move stuff like we would a raccoon.

Mom comes back ten minutes later with a proud smile on her face and a huge white box in her arms. The box is wrapped in several layers of plastic and, as my mom drops it on the coffee table in front of us, a cloud of dust puffs up. Abigail and I suffer the worst of it. Coughing and spluttering, I fan the air away from my face.

"Ah, well," Mom says. "It's been in storage for many years, so a little dust is normal."

She peels off the first layer of plastic, the second, and the third, to reveal the box in all its white splendor. The golden Bluewater Springs Bridal writing shines intact in the firelight. And there goes my last hope mice would've eaten the damn thing, so I wouldn't be forced to try the outdated frock on. Mom sets the plastic aside and turns the box toward me.

"Open it, Honeybun."

I study the lid without touching it. "Mom, I really don't think this is a good idea."

"Don't be silly, it's just a dress. It won't bite you."

With my luck these days, it probably will.

Reluctantly, I take off the lid and move aside various layers of protective wrapping tissue to uncover the eyesore underneath. Oh, gosh, the dress is even worse than I remembered from the pictures.

Mom can't resist and pulls it and all its excess fabric out of the box to reveal the Gownster in all its horror.

"Of course, the gown will need a little restyling, but the fabric and lace detailing are still intact. This was your Grandma Mabel's dress." Tears surface in Mom's eyes. "I had it adapted to marry your father, and now you will make it your own to marry Chuck. The Warren women all getting married in the same gown passed down from mother to daughter."

I stare at the dress again. Even if I had any intention of actually marrying Chuck, which I don't, I'm pretty sure no amount of tailoring could make that thing wearable.

"Mom, I'm not sure using your dress is a good idea."

"The hashtag #mymomsdress is very popular on Instagram," Josiane Masson pipes up. "Many modern brides choose an environmentally-conscious attitude toward fashion where fabrics are repurposed instead of being put to waste. Something old rather than something new will give The Bluewater Springs Chocolate Company brand a real green boost."

"What does the wedding have to do with the company?" I ask.

"Well, the wedding could play an important part in the rebranding. The company already dominates the niche of premium chocolates in the kids' market. But we want to expand the appeal to adults and make it a true family brand." Josiane pauses, and stares at Abigail. "At least, that's how I understood the brief?"

Chuck's mom smiles. "I couldn't have said it better."

"So," Josiane continues, "the Chucokate launch will be the first aggressive play into the adults' market for Valentine's Day, but the wedding could be the real market push. I suggest doing it in winter, since it's the bestselling season for chocolate. And would you consider the actual factory to host the ceremony?"

She doesn't mean *this* winter, does she?

"Isn't it premature to discuss venues?" I ask, a bit desperately.

Miss Influencer ignores my objections and moves along with her marketing pitch. "The town square would be a magnificent spot, too, as long as the candy shop could be featured in the background and maybe the gift shop, too—harder to do in winter, though. And Lillian, would you and Bud consider expanding the Chucokate brand to include a white chocolate variant that we could bring to market as the bridal line?"

"Aw, Josiane, that's a marvelous idea." Mom frowns, taken up in a creative moment. "We would have to adjust the acidity to compensate for the higher sweetness of the white chocolate, but I could definitely see it working."

"I don't even know if I want to get married in white," I sulk.

"Then we'll dye the chocolate and the dress whatever color you choose," Mom says, waving her hand to dismiss my concerns. "Now, stop being such a spoilsport and go put the dress on."

Everyone else cheers at this idea, so I have no other choice than to take the Gownster from my mom and stomp up to my room to change.

I yank my clothes off while whispering more death threats to Chuck. When he gets back, I'm going to use all this lace to strangle him.

To find the right hole to put my feet in, I have to shuffle through various layers of fabric. Then I struggle awhile to pull up the zipper. And, finally, I can step in front of the mirror.

Oh my gosh, someone take my eyes out. The Gownster is hideous, the perfect mix between The Little Mermaid and Diana's wedding gowns. And while both were princesses and female icons, their sense of fashion leaves something to be desired in modern days.

I really don't want anyone to see me wearing this.

"Honeybun!" Mom shouts from downstairs. "What's taking you so long?"

Oh, will they just back the hell off?

Gathering up my skirts, I march out of the room and down the stairs to plant myself squarely in the center of the living room. I swear, if someone dares say this looks good, I'm going to scream.

"Well, yeah," Mom says. "The sleeves might require a little work."

"But the fabric is superb quality," Abigail encourages. "You can tell the lacework is expensive."

Nana Fern sighs contentedly, while Josiane raises her

phone and starts snapping photos.

"Why are you taking pictures?" I ask.

"For any wedding dress makeover, it's important to present before and after shots."

"Well, sorry, but not everything is about business. And I'd prefer no one saw me wearing this."

"No, you're right, Honeybun," Mom says. "Love is the most important part of a wedding. But trust me, even if we don't use the photos in the campaign, you'll want as many keepsakes of these happy times as you can get."

Happy times. Right.

Josiane lowers her phone and stops taking pictures, but the damage is done. She must've already taken a thousand.

"Can I go change now?" I ask defeatedly.

"Yes, go, Honeybun," Mom says. "But try to enjoy yourself a little. Weddings don't have to be stressful."

"Then don't stress me about doing things I don't want to do."

"All right, all right. Go get changed, so we can decide how to spread the news. But be quick this time, I need to get started on dinner soon."

"What do you mean 'spread the news'? I told you I'm not ready to make any plans yet."

"About the wedding, certainly not. But the engagement is a different story. We need to let all our friends and family know, plus plan the engagement party. Since you and Chuck will be home only for another three weeks, I was thinking of doing it just after New Year's…"

My mouth goes dry. Until now, I hadn't realized how serious the situation has become. Because if telling our families Chuck and I broke up was hard, imagine explaining to the entire town why we broke off our engagement. What a nightmare.

"Mom, why don't we hold off on the announcement for a few days? Let people enjoy Christmas, and we can let them know afterward."

"But, Honeybun, if we're going to throw a party, the guests will need to know ahead of time to organize their schedules."

I'm thinking of a believable reason to postpone the announcement when my phone pings with one, two, three… The messages just keep coming. My stomach sinks as Mom's phone and Abigail's start going off as well. This can't be good.

I fight with the skirt, underskirts, and excessive ruffles to reach my bag on the couch and take out my phone.

Fifteen new notifications, and more pouring in. I open one at random.

Congratulations!

I scroll through a few others.

Oh, Kate, so excited for you and Chuck ♥♥♥

I heard the good news, I couldn't be happier for you guys

I'm so happy for you and Chuck

All texts are the same. You and Chuck. You and Chuck. Happy. Happy. Happy. Blah, blah, blah… congratulations!

How did the news get out? It must've been either Chuck or Josiane who spilled the beans. It has to be. And if it was Chuck, I'm not going to be able to marry him in this monstrosity of a dress because I'll already be in jail for his murder.

I turn to the moms. "Who talked?"

"Not me," Mom says.

"How did they find out?"

Abigail checks her phone. "Let me ask Margaret," she says, referring to The Chocolate Company's social media manager.

We wait for a few heartbeats, during which more notifications rain upon us, until Abigail says, "Oh! Apparently, Chuck has made an unofficial announcement at The Plough and Harrow. He was celebrating with his friends and the news spread." She looks up. "I guess that saves us from the family politics game of whom to tell first, right? Everyone knows already!"

"See?" Mom says, addressing me. "Chuck has the right spirit. Be happy, celebrate, tell the world."

That's the last straw. What is Chuck playing at? He must've gone stinking crazy mad!

I'm uttering the ultimate death threat in my head when the sound of footsteps approaches. I raise my gaze and meet the eyes of a shocked—and now very much terrified—Chuck.

Nine

Chuck

Half an hour ago...

With all eyes on me, The Plough and Harrow suddenly becomes too crowded. Soon, my fellow patrons will break the last barrier and come over to congratulate me in person, and I don't want to have to lie to even more people. Plus, being the center of attention makes me uncomfortable, especially when I owe it to a fake engagement to my ex, who I still haven't gotten over and who's dating someone else. I have to get out of this pub—*fast.*

I invent an excuse, say goodbye to my friends, and extricate my way through the crowd. I swear, a football player would have an easier time crossing the field to run a touchdown. The "well-wishers" do everything in their power not to let me out. They grab my hands in congratulatory handshakes, give me shoulder pats, and the bolder ones go for a hug or a kiss on the cheek. Every human interaction, short of actually being tackled to the floor of the pub, I have to endure. But I finally reach the door.

The chilly night air is refreshing. I take a few deep breaths and try to keep my cool. Now that I'm out, the prospect of actually going home and having to face Kate is not promising either. I stare at the mostly empty street and consider my options.

For the first time, I'm grateful Bluewater Springs doesn't have an airport; otherwise, the temptation to hop on a plane and just disappear would've been too great.

"Hey, Chuck," someone calls from across the street. I look up and see Dean, one of the factory workers, coming my way with a big smile on his face. He stops next to me and grabs my hand. "Just heard the news. Congratulations!"

The gossip is spreading faster than I imagined. I have to go home and warn Kate. She's going to kill me this time, I know it. She'll do it tonight in my sleep.

"Thanks, Dean," I say. He looks like he's going to start asking questions about the engagement, so I hastily change the subject. "But hey, shouldn't I be the one congratulating you? Mom told me your team won the production excellence award again. What is it now, three years in a row?"

"Yeah," Dean says proudly, "and we're excited to get started on the Chucokate. The new machines should arrive just after Christmas."

I blink. "New machines?"

"Yeah, we're updating lines three and four. Didn't Mr. Rose tell you? Your parents made a huge investment, but no product has ever had such a high projected positive response as the Chucokate. Everyone is counting on it being a huge success."

My head is reeling with this news, but I manage a response. "Kate and I only got home last night. We didn't have time to catch up yet." It's my turn for a shoulder pat. "I'll let you go inside, Dean, I don't want you to freeze off a few steps away from a well-deserved pint. And if I don't see you again before the twenty-fifth, Merry Christmas."

"Merry Christmas, Chuck, and give a hug to Kate from me as well."

"Uh, yeah. Sure thing."

Despite the sobering low temperatures, I'm still too fresh on the beers to drive home. I hurry away from the pub on foot before any more well-wishers accost me, headed toward Bluewater Bridge. The Warrens live only a ten-minute walk from the pub, so it isn't too far.

As I force myself to walk double-time to keep warm, I reflect on this new unwelcome discovery about the family business. How much did the upgraded machinery cost? What will happen when Kate and I come clean about our breakup? Is it too late—or even possible—to hire actors to be brand ambassadors in our place?

And, most important of all: if this Chucokate campaign crashes and burns because of Kate and me… What happens to the company?

Our parents are too business savvy to bet it all on a single project. But it's clear they've spent a lot—like, a *lot*—on the Chucokate. If the Chucokate fails, the company's financial outlook is probably going to change from stellar to grim.

By the time I walk up the Warrens' driveway, my head isn't any clearer—in fact, it's more muddled than ever—and my hands and feet are about to fall off from the cold. I can't wait to warm them by the fireplace. I hop up the front steps and hurry inside, not bothering to ring the bell since the Warrens' door is always open to me. Besides, they have the most obnoxious-sounding buzzer with a million bells chiming for a good twenty seconds. Gives me a headache every time I hear it.

I head straight for the living room without taking off my jacket in the hall—I'm still too shivery. Then stop dead when I spot Kate standing in the center of the room, wearing a grotesque white gown with an enormous skirt and even bigger sleeves. She looks like a cream puff. Surrounding her, scattered on the two couches and assorted armchairs, are Mom, Lillian, Nana Fern, Kate's aunt Muriel and her cousin

Gretchen, and Josiane Masson—who is covertly taking pictures of the bride-to-be while pretending to check her phone.

Kate's head snaps up, and our gazes meet. And I read murder in her big brown eyes.

I'm already scared, but when Kate's mom starts shrieking like a banshee, my heart jumps into my throat.

"Chuck, noooooo! Turn away!" Lillian screams, jumping to her feet and flapping her arms at me. "What are you doing home so early? You can't see the bride in her wedding dress, it's bad luck!"

Wait, the white monstrosity is supposed to be Kate's wedding dress? If the situation weren't so tragic, I'd laugh. But one peek at her still-furious stare informs me I'd better not.

I'm actually glad as Lillian crosses the room and starts unceremoniously herding me back the way I came. "Out, out. Join your dad and Mick in the barn. We'll be ready for dinner in an hour."

Cast out into the icy night, I trudge through the garden, following the narrow shoveled path that leads to the barn. The slim passage, carved in about twenty to twenty-five inches of puffy snow, is slippery as hell in the dark. Still, I hurry over the ice. What's happening inside the house is so scary, I'd risk breaking my neck to escape faster.

Warmth engulfs me once again as I enter Mick's man cave. A huge fire is burning in the fireplace, casting a dancing orange light on the barn's occupants. Dad and Mick are seated on the brown leather couches, staring at the gigantic flat screen mounted on the wall. An NBA game is playing—Charlotte vs Cleveland—and Dad and Mick are intently watching while Pops Teddy lounges by the fire.

"Hi," I greet everyone.

"Hey," Dad says. "Come to watch the game? It just started."

"No, they threw me out of the house. The women are plotting secret wedding stuff and declared me persona non grata."

"Tell us about it," Mick says with a laugh. "We've been exiled all day."

The dads don't look like they've been suffering too much, but I don't call them out on it. Instead, I head toward the fireplace where Pops Teddy is reading a book.

"Ah, Chuck." He places a bookmark between the pages and closes the book on his lap. "Big day."

"You have no idea, Pops." I slowly remove my outer layers and then warm my hands by the fire. The snow begins melting off my boots and forms little puddles on the hardwood floor.

"So, you're about to marry my Kate."

Wow, can't I go more than three minutes before someone mentions her? And is Pops going to give me *the* speech? I was expecting it from Mick, not him.

"Looks like that," I say warily.

"I only have two pieces of advice for you."

"Yeah?"

"Never lie to your wife."

"Okay," I agree. That seems pretty straightforward. "And the other one?"

With a twinkle of mischief in his eyes, Pops Teddy says, "Always keep her happy between the sheets." He winks, then goes back to his book.

And if my cheeks weren't already flushed red from the time I've spent outside, they'd be flaring up now.

I cough awkwardly and stare at the clock mounted on the wall. Another fifty minutes before we're allowed back in the main house for dinner.

Why is it that today, as soon as I enter a room, I can't wait to get out again?

Ten

Kate

Chuck does his best to avoid me all throughout dinner and in the aftermath. But when his parents and Nana Fern leave, and Mom and Dad say goodnight, he has nowhere left to run.

"Why don't we go to bed as well, *Honey?*" I ask in my sweetest, I'm-going-to-murder-you voice.

Chuck sighs and follows me upstairs.

The moment he closes the door, I wheel on him. "Why did you tell the entire town we're engaged? What is *wrong* with you?!"

"It was an accident."

I cross my arms, glaring at him. "You mean to tell me that, in a single day, you've managed to both accidentally propose to me *and* accidentally tell the entire town about it? What's on the agenda for tomorrow: accidentally marrying me over breakfast?"

"I was trying to do damage control," Chuck says. He feeds me a story about his friends thinking I cheated on him at Halloween, and how he had to tell them about the engagement to save my reputation. Then he brings up a new investment our parents made in the factory specifically for the Chucokate.

I sit on the bed and massage my temples as he finally stops talking. The urge to murder him is gone. He's just too sincere in his rambling explanations for all the drama he's caused to be intentional.

"Okay," I eventually say.

He peers at me suspiciously. "Okay? That's it?"

"You could've handled it better, *obviously,* but there's not much we can do about it now. Fact remains that now we're in an even bigger mess than before. We need to set the record straight with both our families *and* the entire town now—and all without ruining the Chucokate brand and costing our parents hundreds of thousands of dollars."

Chuck groans, and flops down on his side of the bed. "It'd be a lot easier if they just chose another couple to represent the stupid Chucokate. There's got to be someone out there better suited to be brand ambassadors than us."

"That could solve the business sides of things, *maybe.* But our parents would still be obsessed about us getting married."

We sit in silence for at least a minute, both lost in our own thoughts. Then, out of the blue, the perfect solution hits me. "That's it!"

"What's it?"

"We've been tackling the problem from the wrong angle. The key is for our parents to *not* want us to be together!"

Chuck turns this over in his mind for a few seconds. "Because if they hated the idea of us as a couple, it'd be a relief rather than a tragedy when we called off the engagement..."

"Plus, they definitely wouldn't want us as their brand ambassadors, which means we'd be off the hook completely."

"The Chucokate would tank," Chuck warns.

I wave my hand at him. "The Chucokate isn't coming out for another two months. There's enough time to adjust the campaign. Maybe it won't be a smashing success, but it won't tank either."

He chews on his lower lip, something he does when he's thinking hard. "So we just have to be the worst couple in the world, without making it obvious what we're doing. How are we supposed to manage that?"

"No clue. Luckily, there's no problem Google can't solve."

I take out my phone and search for the top reasons parents don't like their kids' significant other.

The first search result is a too specific, non-replicable article full of parents complaining about their daughters' boyfriends. "He deflowered my sweet angel... He stole her from us..." Reason number three makes me chuckle. "Listen to this—Over dinner last week, my daughter's Significant Other wouldn't stop talking about *Star Trek*. I've shunned him from the house. Forever."

I glance pointedly at Chuck, and he glowers at me. "I'm obsessed with Star *Wars,* not *Star Trek,*" he notes. "And I know how to carry on a conversation like a normal human being, thank you very much."

"Star Whatever, the quote is still funny."

"You say that because you've never given the movies a fair chance. If you'd only—"

I stop him with a raised hand before he can advocate what an interesting character Jabba the Hutt is. I've seen pictures—big, ugly slug guy. No thank you. "I wasn't interested in your science fiction flicks when we were together, and I'm not interested in them now. Save your breath."

"Your loss."

The next article I find presents a more legitimate list.

"Personality issues... No, that won't work, they adore you. Physical appearance, nope. Socioeconomic status, no. Race, no. Cultural differences, no. Career, no. Oh, for heaven's sake, according to this we're perfect for each other!"

Chuck looks like he's about to say something in response, but he wisely keeps his mouth shut.

Just when I'm about to despair, I read the last line. "Other life choices, like the willingness to start a family. That's it!"

A smile slowly appears on Chuck's face. "Our moms are obsessed with having grandkids."

"Exactly. Imagine how they'd feel if we told them one of us didn't want kids. They'd force us to split up on the spot."

"One problem: you want to tell your mom you don't want to have a baby? Because I sure won't tell mine."

"Hmm… Yeah, that's fair. Okay… What if we *couldn't* have kids?"

"What do you mean?"

"We tell them we did a test on campus, we just got the results back, and you're sterile."

Chuck shakes his head firmly. "Nu-uh, my mom would die of heartbreak, and so would yours. And besides, they'd just insist we adopt or something. It wouldn't solve a thing."

"No, you're right." I deflate. "But we need to find a solution. This situation is making me sick to my stomach."

I rack my brain a little longer but exclude one possibility after the other… unless… "Of course, the easiest thing would be to tell them you cheated on me, they wouldn't force me to take you back after that. And that's why you proposed, so I'd forgive you, and I said yes because I got lost in the romance of the moment, but then once my mind cooled off I realized we're no longer right for each other. It would make total sense."

Chuck scoffs. "Yeah, right."

"What's that supposed to mean?"

"That if we must invent an affair, you should be the

cheater."

"Why?"

"Because you started dating Marco, what, a week after you dumped me? Plus, a rumor is already spreading around town that you cheated on me, so it'd be perfect."

Anger heats my cheeks. "Just so we're clear, I did *not* cheat on you."

"I'm not saying you did. But you have to admit you moved on at light speed."

I don't owe him explanations, and I'm done with this conversation. "We'll figure it out tomorrow. I'm going to bed."

"Fine. I need to use the bathroom anyway." Chuck storms out of the room.

I grab a pillow, smoosh it against my face, and scream into it.

Eleven

Lillian

"Honey, I can't sleep," I tell Mick, tossing in bed.

"Is something the matter?"

"My back is killing me."

"If you want a massage, you don't have to put up such an act, just ask."

"Mick, I'm being serious, my spine isn't properly aligned. I should try that knee pillow thingy again."

"Oh, Lilly, when will you stop buying everything you see on infomercials? Are misaligned spines even a real thing?"

"They are because I have one, and I was talking with Dorothy Brown the other day, and she swore the knee pillow works. I must've been too quick in dismissing it. I'll go grab it from the storeroom."

"All right, Sweetheart, just promise you won't spend the night kicking me in the shins."

"I promise."

I kiss my husband on the nose and get out of bed.

The storeroom is adjoining to Kate's room and, from the hall, I can hear the kids' voices inside. I still remember the days when Mick and I would stay up all night talking. Well, not *just* talking. Ah, young love.

I open the storeroom door and grope to find the pull wire switch lamp—another one of my infomercial purchases that actually comes in handy. My fingers finally close around the wire and I pull on it. The lamp comes to life—just about. I must've forgotten to change the batteries. I make a mental note to do that tomorrow. But for now, the lamp produces enough light for me to search the back rack where I should've stacked the knee foam support pillow. Ah, there it is on the bottom shelf.

I grab the pillow, and I'm about to leave when I overhear Kate's voice in the other room enunciate the word "grandkids" clear as day.

I pause and, I know I shouldn't, but I lean closer to the bedroom wall. The voices aren't exactly distinct; I can only make out a few words of what Chuck is saying in response.

"…to tell Mom… have a baby…"

Oh, dear me… is Kate pregnant? Am I about to become a grandma?

"…we did a test on campus… results… and you're virile."

Virile? Is that what Kate said? I can't be sure. But it must be. My Honeybun took a pregnancy test, and it was positive.

Chuck mumbles something I can't discern. Kate replies, but I only catch the ending.

"…is making me sick to my stomach."

So *that's* why she looked so pale all day, and why she stomped around in such a horrendous mood this afternoon. Now it all adds up: she has morning sickness. How many weeks along is she?

"Sweetheart, are you okay?"

Mick's voice makes me jump.

"Shhhh!" I grab my husband and pull him into the storeroom, closing the door behind him. Without the light coming from the corridor, the wire lamp is doing an even poorer job, and we're in semi-darkness.

"What are you doing?" Mick asks, understandably confused.

"Eavesdropping on Kate and Chuck."

"I'm not sure you should—"

"Kate is pregnant, Mick. We're going to be grandparents!"

His smile lights up the storeroom better than the wire lamp ever could. "Really? When? How?"

Hands on my hips, I stare my husband down. "Mick Warren, do I really have to explain to you *how?*"

Mick pulls me into an embrace and nuzzles my neck. "Actually, I wouldn't mind a practical lesson. I bet it would also solve all your back problems, too."

I kiss him on the lips, and we get a little carried away. Until the kids mention a name on the other side.

"Did they say Margot?" I ask Mick. "Oh my gosh, they're having a baby girl!"

Mick ignores my deductions and goes back to kissing my neck, and I stop paying attention to the kids and concentrate on my husband.

Twelve

Chuck

When I step out of Kate's room, giggling sounds erupt from the linen closet in front of the bathroom. For a moment I think I've imagined it, but then I hear another noise. There's definitely someone—or something—in there.

"Hello? Is anyone in there?"

I'm not sure what I'm expecting to find when I open the door, but it's certainly not Kate's parents, in their pajamas, making out in the semi-darkness like a couple of horny teenagers. Lillian spots me and squeaks like a mouse while her husband is still trying to kiss her. I stammer something incomprehensible and then flee back into the safety of Kate's bedroom.

She's lying on the bed with a pillow pressed over her face.

When I close the door, Kate removes the pillow and raises an eyebrow at me. "That was quick."

"I never made it to the bathroom."

"Got lost?"

"Ha ha. No, I caught your parents making out in the storage closet. They looked one minute away from tearing their clothes off."

"Oh. Eww. Gross."

She covers her face with the pillow again, and I sag onto the bed next to her, wondering if the image of Lillian and Mick entwined in a passionate embrace will stay branded in my brain forever.

"Well," I say. "At least it looks like your dad is following Pops' marital advice."

Kate ditches the pillow and turns to me. "Meaning?"

"Today, Teddy told me the secret to a happy marriage is twofold: never lie to your wife, and always take care of her in bed."

Kate pats me on the shoulder sarcastically. "You had one of those nailed down, but you might want to work on the other one for your next relationship."

"I never lied to you," I protest, outraged.

She arches her eyebrows pointedly. "No, I know, I was referring to the other thing."

I scowl. "Are you saying I was lousy in bed?"

"No." She shrugs. "Just not much interested in having sex."

"Not interested in having sex? When was I not interested in sex? I'm all for sex."

"Not when you're playing your stupid video games on the PlayStation."

I can't help but laugh at the idea of ever turning down sex for a video game. "Fine, maybe I didn't want to quit a record game halfway through to go to some boring vernissage of modern art neither of us understands. But if you'd presented me with the alternative of sex, I would've thrown my best Final Fantasy top score through the window without a second thought."

"No, you wouldn't have. I tested it."

"What do you mean, you *tested* it?" Why do I feel like every conversation I've had with her in the past four months *has been recorded for training and quality purposes?*

"I tried the towel test. You failed."

She's officially lost me. "What's a towel test?"

"It's simple. If you think your boyfriend's more interested in video games than you, you walk past him wearing only a towel, then drop the towel to the floor." She pulls up a video on her phone and hands it to me. "This is how you *should* have reacted."

I watch a montage of guys abandoning their controllers at the speed of light to follow their girlfriends like overeager puppies. One guy is so excited, he forgets he has headphones on and gives himself such a bad whiplash with the cable that he falls on his bum.

"Guess how you reacted?" Kate says, then mimics me pushing buttons on an imaginary controller with eyes fixed on an invisible screen.

"Kate, I swear on my life, you never stepped in front of me and dropped no towel to no floor."

"Yes, I did. I told you I was taking a shower and dropped the towel."

"Did I even see you?" I protest. "Because if I had, I wouldn't have been..." I mimic her me-playing-video-games motion.

I drop the act and stare her dead in the eyes. "The visual element is fundamental for this test, and since I didn't see you, the test is invalid. Because, Kate, I swear, if you were ever to walk in front of me naked except for a towel, and drop said towel to the floor, I would quit every other activity immediately and have sex with you in a heartbeat."

Okay, maybe that came out a little strong. Especially considering we aren't together anymore. But, come on, the idea that I would ever choose video games over Kate is simply absurd.

I can read the weirdness on her face, so I quickly follow up with a joke. "Of course, I might have to forget how you looked wearing that white monstrosity of a wedding dress from earlier."

Kate smiles. "How dare you mock me about it, after the afternoon I had to endure?"

"At least Nana Fern didn't offer you dirty marriage advice."

She makes to playfully swat me, but I catch her hand and don't let go. We stare into each other's eyes, and my heartrate skyrockets. This is the Kate I used to know, the Kate I still can't believe left me. She must read the thought in my expression, because she pulls back.

"I'm with Marco," she says.

"I know."

A heavy, loaded silence follows.

I break it first. "Is that one of the reasons you broke up with me? Because you thought I didn't want you anymore?"

"Among other things…"

"What things?"

"That you showed no interest in anything I cared about, or that you wouldn't even consider London… It seemed obvious we wanted different things and that our lives were moving in opposite directions."

"And Marco is coming to London?"

"I've only been dating Marco for a few months. And besides, he isn't the—" She abruptly cuts herself off.

"The?" I prompt.

"Never mind."

"When?" I say. "When did you stop loving me, Kate?"

"Chuck, that's not—" She sighs. "Please don't ask me that."

Right, I've had enough of this conversation for one night.

"I still need the bathroom," I say. "The coast should be clear by now."

I leave the bedroom. Kate doesn't stop me. Thankfully, in

the hall everything is silent. Her parents must've taken their extracurricular activities to the bedroom. Why they were doing it in the closet in the first place will stay a mystery.

When I come back from brushing my teeth, Kate is already under the covers, sleeping. Or at least, she's pretending to. I climb in beside her and pretend to do the same.

Thirteen

Kate

I stub my toe on the way to the window the next morning, and curse under my breath so as not to wake Chuck.

Snow is swirling beyond the glass, and I'm not that committed to my training to brave the elements. Instead, I pull on a knit Chocolate Company Christmas sweater featuring a snowman and our bestselling knit slipper boots with a white faux-fur interior. No wonder we run out of inventory for the boots every single holiday season; my feet feel like they just entered a cozy, warm winter spa.

Most of the things I wear at home are merchandise from the chocolate factory, which expands well beyond ugly Christmas sweaters. Since we've started working with freelance designers, our apparel line has stepped up a notch. And I have to admit, Chuck is the mastermind behind that success. No matter how demanding grad school gets, he supervises all the new products and gives Abigail the final go-ahead. So far, everything he's okayed has been a success.

Watching him sleep now, I remember how different our mornings used to be. Playful, caring, affectionate. Steamy, sometimes, especially when we first moved in together.

But those times are gone. Time to move on.

A subversive battalion of butterflies mounts a protest in my belly. Apparently, the love bugs don't agree with my decision to break it off with Chuck. Our honest conversation last night has left me a little raw. Not to mention how confidently Chuck said he'd have sex with me in a heartbeat, like it was never in doubt. His eyes were practically eating me up as he said it, like I was a particularly delicious treat ready to be devoured.

It was enough to make me wonder if Chuck really didn't see me that night. Is it possible to get so focused on something you don't notice your girlfriend parading naked in front of you? It just seems so ridiculous, and yet… The way he was looking at me…

If not for Marco, I'm pretty sure Chuck and I would have had sex last night. But, thankfully, I have a boyfriend, which has saved me from the inevitably awkward morning after, and from having to kick myself for relapsing with my ex. I can't get sloppy in this breakup. Leaving Chuck was the hardest thing I've ever done; I don't know if I could summon the strength to do it twice.

Our lives are moving on divergent paths; I have to remember that. Chuck can't wait to finish school and move back home. He's looking forward to spending all his evenings at The Plough and Harrow with his friends, while all I can think about is London. At least getting over him will become easier once we've got an ocean separating us.

As I exit the bedroom, the wonderful fragrance of Mom's cooking wraps around me like a warm blanket. Mmm, fresh baked goods. My stomach growls in response, and I hop down the stairs and join her in the kitchen.

"Morning, Mom," I say, playfully bumping butts with her.

"Good morning, Honeybun," she greets me with a radiant smile.

The bright welcome is a nice change of attitude from last night's sulky side stares—she wasn't happy with me after the scarce enthusiasm I showed for the Gownster. But I guess all the storeroom sex with my dad turned her mood around.

"What are you cooking?" I ask, sitting on a stool at the

island. "Smells delicious."

"Gingerbread cookies, with a little extra ginger." She waltzes between the oven and the kitchen island, removing one tray of baked gingerbread men and putting a fresh tray in. Then she hands me a plate with a warm cookie. "Want to try one? Ginger is a fantastic natural remedy to settle a queasy stomach."

I don't have a queasy stomach, but I don't need an excuse to eat my mom's fresh-out-of-the-oven cookies.

I grab the little man and break off his legs, arms, and head to make them cool faster. One last blow, and I bite the head in half.

"Mmm, Mom," I say with my mouth still full. "This is delicious."

Mom stares at me eagerly. Perhaps too eagerly. "And how are you feeling this morning?"

"Okay, I guess."

"No nausea?"

"No, Mom." What's with her and the nausea? Do I look exhausted or something? I didn't exactly sleep well. Maybe I should have freshened up before coming downstairs.

"You don't have to pretend around me, Honeybun. A mother can sense certain things."

"What things?"

"That you and Chuck are having a baby!"

"What?" I half choke on the gingerbread man's head, and sputter crumbs all over the island. "I'm not pregnant, Mom!"

"I know it's considered bad luck to tell anyone before the end of the first trimester, but I'm not superstitious."

"Well, that's good, because I'm not pregnant. And besides, it's not about superstition—people wait until the first trimester is over because that's when the majority of spontaneous miscarriages occur."

"Look at you, already the expert. Come on, you can talk to me."

"There's nothing to talk about." Where did she even get such a crazy idea?

"Deny it all you want." She beats a wooden spoon over the batter bowl. "But I overheard you talking with Chuck last night. I didn't mean to, of course, it just happened."

I must go pale, because she runs to my side.

"Oh, Honeybun, don't worry, there's nothing to be ashamed of."

"Mom, you must've heard wrong."

"No, I didn't. You were talking with Chuck about having a baby, that you felt sick, and that you didn't know how to tell us after you did a test on campus. So really, Honeybun, you can quit the secrecy act."

I'm starting to get desperate now. "Mom, there's no secrecy act because there's no secret."

"If you're not pregnant, then what else could you and Chuck possibly be keeping from us that's making you sick to your stomach?"

My brain tries to speed-shuffle through possible answers to that question. Anything but the truth. But of course, I blank out, and words escape me.

Mom whoops, then grabs me in a bone-crushing hug. "I knew it! Oh, congratulations, Sweetheart!"

That's when Chuck enters the kitchen, looking impossibly hot-geeky with his hair adorably disheveled and his Christmas elves sweats set on—another of his designs.

Mom doesn't even try to play it cool; she rushes to him and hugs him, saying, "Ah, the father of my grandchild!"

Chuck looks taken aback, and stares at me over Mom's shoulder with a confused expression while patting her on the back.

I wince. "Good news, Honey. Mom knows about the baby. That we're having. Together."

Chuck's face drains of blood. He disentangles himself from my mom's arms and, with an incredibly forced smile, says, "Lillian, do you mind if I talk in private with Kate for a second?"

"Oh, don't be mad at her for spilling the beans," Mom says. "I'd already found out on my own."

"I'd still like to have a word."

He walks over to me, grabs my hand, and all but drags me out of the kitchen.

Once more, we end up locked up in my room.

"A baby, Kate?" he demands. "As if things weren't hard enough already! What were you thinking?"

"Shhhh," I say. "Mom is probably eavesdropping again."

"A baby?" Chuck repeats, shout-whispering.

"It's not my fault!" I snap. "And as if you can talk after that stupid proposal and the mess you made in town last night."

"But… why? How?"

"Because Mom is a great multitasker apparently, and she managed to have sex in the closet with my dad and spy on us at the same time. She heard us talking about babies, and a test we took on campus, and that we didn't know how to tell them, and that I was sick, and she concluded a baby is on the way."

Chuck digs both his hands into his hair. "This is a disaster."

"Don't be so dramatic. We're already fake engaged. Why should a fake baby be any worse?"

Fourteen

Chuck

We find out the answer to Kate's question later that afternoon as we sit in Pastor Grant's office listening to how modern and broad-minded our parents are.

In the span of only a few hours, everything's gone to Hell in a handbasket. Lillian told my parents about the fake baby while Kate and I were upstairs arguing, which resulted in a big, celebratory meal—and before we could even finish digesting it, Kate and I were marched to church.

Pastor Grant sits patiently behind his desk, pulling at his chin as our parents ramble on about the many *liberal* reasons we should push the wedding forward. They've assembled in attack formation in a semicircle of four chairs in front of the desk, while Kate and I follow the exchange from a bench on the sidelines.

"Of course, Pastor, we're not prudes," Lillian is saying. "Or old-fashioned. But it'd be preferable if the kids got married before the baby came. Life with a newborn can be difficult, and the last thing they'll want on their plates is a wedding to organize. And if they got married now, they'd also have a chance at a real honeymoon, just the two of them. Although, Kate, you still haven't told us how many weeks along you are. Will you be able to travel?"

"Not sure, Mom," Kate says between gritted teeth.

"Well, we can figure that out, of course. And it would be better if they got married before the bump started to show. Pastor, you know how mean the gossip can get, especially in small towns. How soon can the ceremony take place?"

Pastor Grant leans his elbows on the table and scrutinizes the parents. “Are you sure a shotgun wedding is what your son and daughter want?”

“Shotgun wedding?” Mick says, offended. “No, no. This would be just *a* wedding. The kids have been together for so long, they’re in love, and we only want what’s best for them.”

“Yeah, you said that already,” Pastor Grant replies, visibly annoyed. As for me, I wished they’d stop calling us *the kids*. “Does the baby have a name?”

“Margot,” Lillian says happily. “It’s a girl.”

I raise an eyebrow at Kate, and she shrugs in a I-have-no-idea-where-that-came-from way.

“A baby girl,” the pastor says pensively. “A new life is always welcome in the community, and if Chuck and Kate wish to get married, there are a few formalities to complete. But I believe we can arrange it.”

“How soon?” my mom asks eagerly.

“Would next Friday work?” Lillian presses.

“Next Friday?” Kate asks, eyes bulging.

“Yes, Honeybun, imagine it! Getting married on New Year’s Eve; wouldn’t that be wonderful?” And without waiting for a reply, she turns back to the pastor. “Is a week long enough to execute all the formalities?”

“It should suffice,” Pastor Grant says. “Now, if you don’t mind, I’d like to have a word with Kate and Chuck in private.”

The parents oblige and mumble a series of goodbyes as they shuffle out of the office.

“Thank you, Pastor.”

“See you tonight at the midnight mass.”

“Looking forward to your sermon.”

Lillian closes the door behind her, leaving me and Kate alone under the stern gaze of the pastor.

He gestures at the now-empty chairs before his desk, and we dutifully move into the direct line of fire.

"As I'm sure you know, getting married is not an endeavor to be taken lightly," the pastor intones. "Marriage is not easy, and even couples who embark on this lifelong journey with the best of intentions might fall short. Yes, you're about to become parents, but that can't be the sole reason to make such a commitment. Baby Margot will be loved and cherished no matter your marital status. You shouldn't let external pressures from your parents decide for you."

We both nod, but neither of us speaks.

So the pastor continues with his lecture. "Now, before I can in good conscience bring you to the altar, we need to schedule at least one session of premarital counseling. With my other couples the course usually takes much longer, but, given the situation, I feel like we can cover the essential with a single meeting."

Kate and I stare at each other, then back at Pastor Grant, at a loss for words.

"Has the cat eaten your tongues?" Pastor Grant asks.

"Err..." I clear my throat. "Pastor, what if we agreed with you, and weren't sure getting married was the right choice for us? Would you help us tell our parents?"

His gaze turns even more severe. "Chuck, Kate, free will is every man or woman's prerogative." He lets his eyes rest on me, and then Kate. "But can I make a suggestion?"

We both nod, and Kate smiles hopefully, "Yes, please, Pastor."

"If you want your parents to stop treating you like a

couple of bratty children, then start behaving like the two adults you both are and tell them you don't want to get married."

"Ah." Kate's hopeful smile turns to a grimace. "So, when did you say you wanted to schedule our session?"

***

"Why did you have to make an actual appointment for a premarital course?" I ask, as we walk back to Kate's house. "We both agree we're not getting married, right?"

"Of course, not," Kate scoffs. "But you know our mothers, they're probably going to call the pastor to make sure everything is on schedule for Friday. If we'd confessed everything to Pastor Grant, he would've told them, and unless that's how you wanted our parents to find out..."

"That might've actually been a good idea. Let the pastor do the dirty work while we sit back and watch."

"You wishing we'd come clean in September as much as I am?"

"I don't think it's possible to wish any harder than I've been doing."

We walk in silence for a few minutes, crunching our way through the fresh-fallen snow. Eventually, Kate speaks up again. "What do we do about the Chucokate?"

"The more I think about it the more I'm convinced the only way out is to hire professional actors to become the face of the campaign instead of us. Which means we need to talk to Josiane Masson and ask her if that's likely to work as a marketing strategy."

"Chuck, that's genius. This way the launch would go ahead anyway, our parents wouldn't lose the investment for the rebranding and the marketing campaign, and we'd be free."

"It could really work if we managed to get Josiane on board. When is our next meeting with her? Is she staying for Christmas?"

"Chuck, do you ever listen to anything anyone tells you?"

"Yes, why?"

She rolls her eyes. "We have a photo shoot planned with her in," Kate stares at her watch. "Oh, gosh, in an hour, and we were supposed to be home fifteen minutes ago for hair and makeup. Come on, let's hurry."

Kate grabs my hand and drags me forward, speeding up her pace.

"Okay, okay, I'm coming," I say as I hurry after her. "But I'm not putting on makeup!"

Fifteen

Kate

"Chuck, please put both your arms around Kate's waist," Josiane directs us while the photographer, Louis, snaps shot after shot of me and Chuck together.

Mom's kitchen is acting as the set, and Chuck and I look as if The Bluewater Springs Chocolate Company apparel store has exploded on us. Everything's factory branded, from the shirts on our backs to the pot holders on the counter. But the cheesiest items by far are the his and hers aprons we're wearing, decorated with male and female cartoon reindeer. Another one of Chuck's designs.

Also, Chuck *is* wearing makeup. It's barely noticeable, but he's still fuming about it. And why does he have to be so cute when he broods?

They did my makeup first, and while the makeup artist was struggling to apply the thinnest layer of contouring to his skin, Josiane and I went through our winter catalog to pick outfits. And I was overwhelmed by the number of new products Chuck has brought to market. I always accused him of doing nothing other than play games, but where did he find the time to draw all these unique characters while still keeping excellent grades in school? Perhaps I haven't been fair with him.

Also, why is apparel generally categorized as ugly Christmas wear making him ten times hotter than normal?

It's not fair.

And looks aren't even the worst part; the tactile aspect of all these poses we have to switch through is quickly becoming impossible to cope with. And it's about to get worse. As Chuck follows Josiane's instructions and hugs me from behind, my body temperature soars to fever levels, and not just because we're standing near the lit oven.

"Wonderful," Josiane encourages. "Now, Chuck, move your hands on Kate's belly as if you were caressing her baby bump."

"I don't have a baby bump," I protest.

"You will soon, and we want to document all stages of the pregnancy."

Kill. Me. Now.

"Is this okay?" Chuck whispers in my ear, his breath a warm, distracting caress down my neck. "If you want to stop, I reckon she got enough pictures."

"No, let's do as she says and get this over with."

I grab Chuck's hands and place them on my belly.

"Perfect," Josiane says. "That's even better, keep holding hands. Chuck, bend a little and kiss her neck."

Behind me, Chuck stiffens, so I squeeze his hands to let him know it's okay.

Soft lips press on my skin a few seconds later, searing a burning patch in that spot just below my ear Chuck knows makes me lose my mind. Did he do it on purpose? Or was it an involuntary reflex to kiss me there out of habit?

"Hold… hold…" Josiane instructs.

If she doesn't make us change positions soon, I'm going to ignite like a sparkler and begin to emit flashes of light. Which is weird, because Chuck hasn't made me so hot and bothered in ages. My skin is tingling, my pulse is speeding, and, again, if Marco wasn't in my life, once this photo shoot was over I'd probably drag Chuck to my bedroom and—let's leave it there.

Is that why people often end up having sex with their exes after they've broken up? Because it feels safe but prohibited, new but familiar, wrong but right? I don't know. Chuck has been my only serious boyfriend and my only serious breakup. Could it be that, since I'm not supposed to want him anymore, Chuck has become the forbidden fruit, and that's why I've developed all these dirty fantasies about him?

Whatever the reason, if the air turns any steamier in this kitchen, I might turn into a dumpling.

"Okay, Chuck, thank you, you can straighten up." Chuck follows the directions, letting go of me, and suddenly I feel colder than if I was running around the backyard in my underwear. "No, no, no," Josiane hurries to add. "Keep your arms around Kate."

He hugs me again from behind, and I'm ashamed to be relieved his arms are back around me.

"Now, Kate," Josiane continues. "Dirty your hand with some flour and smear it across Chuck's nose as you stare up at him adoringly. We're going for playful and romantic, so don't be afraid to have some fun with it."

I do as instructed, even if it was ten times easier to deal with the awkwardness without the added stress of eye contact. I've always adored Chuck's deep blue eyes and, apparently, the breakup hasn't changed the effect they have on me. Not when he looks at me like I'm the only person in the room. Heck, the only woman in the whole wide world.

My heart skips a beat, then positively stops as Josiane utters the next instruction: "And now kiss."

Chuck's eyes widen in panic, as well as some other emotion I can't place.

"Is it really necessary?" I ask, looking at her. "We're not that comfortable with PDAs."

Josiane huffs impatiently. “I’m asking you guys for a peck on the lips not to make out in front of the camera. You’ll have to kiss in front of people at your wedding; might as well start getting used to it.”

With a heavy sigh, I turn back to Chuck and nod.

He closes his eyes and presses his lips on mine in the softest kiss ever. *Gosh, I missed his lips,* is the first treacherous thought that crosses my mind.

“Fantastic, guys, don’t move. Louis needs to shoot a few different angles. And relax, please, you’re both too rigid. Kate, reach up with your right hand and bury it in Chuck’s hair.”

I do as I’m told and, oh, gosh, Chuck’s soft hair is my other great weakness after his eyes. I can’t help but move my fingers between his silken dark locks while my other hand tightens on Chuck’s. In response, he pulls me in closer to his body from behind, positively knocking the breath out of me.

“All right,” Josiane says. “I think we have it.”

We pull apart, breaking the kiss, but remaining in each other’s arms. Chuck stares down at me in wonder, and a deeper emotion he tries to hide. Could it be longing? And I don’t know how I’m staring back at him, but it must be equally intense, because Josiane cheers, “Yes, yes, yes, don’t move! Keep looking at each other like that. That’s our money shot right there, exactly what true love should look like.”

I push back from Chuck as if electrocuted by Josiane’s words.

“Sorry,” I say, and blab the first excuse that comes to mind. “I’m going to be sick.”

Not even an excuse, as I might actually be sick.

I run out of the kitchen as Josiane comments, “Poor girl. I’ve heard the first trimester can be a real bitch.”

Chuck's reply barely reaches my ears as I rush upstairs. "Right, I'd better go check on her."

His words put a new sprint in my step, and I reach the upstairs bathroom and lock myself in before he can catch up with me.

As I stare in the mirror, my heart is racing in my chest, and not just because of the recent sprint up the staircase.

Fake engagements. Side effects might include nausea, sudden bouts of tachycardia, lust attacks, fever, regrets, confusion, disorientation… longing…

Sixteen

Chuck

"Hey." I knock on the upstairs bathroom door. "Everything all right in there?"

"Yeah," comes Kate's muffled voice from the other side. "But I might be experiencing a hysterical pregnancy."

"You want me to tell Josiane and the photographer to go home? They've taken enough pictures."

"Yes, thank you, I'm not up to do more."

"All right."

I walk back down the stairs and inform everyone Kate is too tired to continue. Josiane is disappointed but tells her crew to start packing up. As they put away the various lighting equipment, I sidle over to her.

"Josiane," I say. "Can I pick your brain about something?"

"Yeah, sure."

"As you probably saw today, Kate isn't comfortable in the spotlight, and, frankly, neither am I. Plus, you said it yourself: the first trimester can be difficult, and Kate could do without the additional stress. Would it make a big difference to hire actors for the rebranding campaign?"

"Actors?"

"Yeah, you know, models who would pose for the photo shoots in our place?"

"That'd be a disaster," Josiane says without a moment's hesitation. "The media is flooded with fakes, and consumers crave authenticity. The Bluewater Springs Chocolate Company is a family brand. You and Kate are the family."

We *are* family, just not in the way everyone assumes. After growing up as close as Kate and I have, not even a breakup could dissolve that bond. But I can't see how we can possibly sell our fake fairytale romance to the masses. Especially not when the lies just keep piling on.

"No, I know, but wouldn't professionals do a better job?"

"Absolutely not." Josiane grabs the photographer's tablet and pulls up a few images from today's shoot. "Look at these," she insists. "You can't fake love like this."

I wish she knew how wrong she was.

I stare at the pictures and die a little inside. Because the photos could pass for real and are a slap in my face. A glimpse at how my life could've been today if I hadn't messed up everything with Kate. If only I'd paid attention.

I drop the tablet and move away. "I'm not saying Kate and I featuring on the campaign isn't the ideal situation. But I don't want to pressure her. What if the morning sickness worsens? What I'm trying to say is, if push came to shove, could professionals substitute us and take over the campaign?"

"I wouldn't recommend it, but, yes, it could be done."

"And what would be the impact?"

Josiane places a hand under her chin, thinking. "I'd say a thirty to fifty percent drop in engagement. Little chance of going viral. Fewer likes, comments, and re-shares would lead to fewer eyeballs on your ads, which in turn would lead to even fewer likes, comments, and re-shares. It's a vicious downward cycle. Organic reach would drop even further…"

So much for that. She's basically saying the campaign would flop. No way I'm doing that to the family business, not after all the work I've put into it.

"Thank you, Josiane," I say resignedly. "We'll take into

consideration everything you said."

"Sure."

"So, are you going home tonight, or…?"

"Oh, no. I'll come back tomorrow morning to arrange the dining room. Your mom showed me some pictures of past Christmases, and Lillian truly did an excellent job with the setting up, but this year we want to raise the bar to make the seating look more professional. I want a picture of your family's Christmas table to be re-pinned on every holiday décor board Pinterest has."

So no telling our parents until at least after Christmas, then, not if Josiane is going to be hovering around all day. Plus Kate and I already sort of agreed to wait until the twenty-sixth to tell our parents our real relationship status. We don't want to spoil Christmas for everybody. And, hopefully, nothing is on the schedule for the day after.

I ask Josiane to make sure.

"What about the twenty-sixth, anything planned for that day?"

"No, I'll take a short break after tomorrow and be back in time for the wedding. And let me tell you, the ceremony will give us some real Pinterest magic. Brides go crazy on that platform."

"I thought you were all about Instagram."

"I'm a visual branding expert," Josiane says. "And Pinterest is key to a long-term strategy. No matter how successful, an Instagram post has a short lifespan. Not to talk about stories, which are limited to twenty-four-hour periods. But pins live on and are researchable and re-pinnable forever."

"Right," I say. "Sorry, I'm not that keen on social media."

She pats my shoulder. "That's why your parents hired me,

to take care of everything. Don't worry, I'll try to make it as easy as I can on you and Kate."

"Thanks," I say. "And, well, see you tomorrow. Merry Christmas."

"Merry Christmas, Chuck, and say goodbye to Kate for me."

Once she's gone, I sit at the island, alone for once. Since we needed Lillian's kitchen for the photo shoot, she and my dad have been cooking at my parents' house this afternoon. We'll have Christmas Eve dinner over there tonight.

I try to reflect on everything that Josiane told me. Are Kate and I being selfish for wanting to derail this campaign? Will the company really be hurt, or would it be just a minor setback? Maybe we could reach a middle ground. Tell our parents about the breakup, but still agree to pose as brand ambassadors. If today's pictures were good enough, I don't see what difference it would make to keep going... other than that we'd be selling a lie...

Well, you know what they say. Fake it until you make it.

***

On Christmas Day, Kate's phone starts vibrating on the bedside table way too early. She rustles under the covers and must grab it, because the dreadful noise of plastic bumping against hardwood stops.

I keep to my side of the bed, turned away from her, and pretend I'm asleep. A bit of a habit lately.

"Hello," she says in a low voice, groggy with sleep, shifting position on the mattress. I can't be sure, but if I had to guess, I'd say she's pulled herself up, half-sitting. "Oh, hi. Merry Christmas."

I can't hear Marco's voice on the other end, but I'm sure

it's him.

"Yes, I was sleeping," she says, and then, as if she needed to justify herself, she adds, "It's Christmas, Marco… No, it isn't an excuse. Listen, I stayed up late last night, I told you it's a tradition that we serve hot chocolate to the entire congregation after midnight mass on Christmas Eve. I didn't go to bed until three in the morning."

Careful not to give the appearance of moving, I slide my left arm closer to my face to read the time on my watch. Given the ungodly hour, light is still scarce, and the glow-in-the-dark numbers have almost entirely faded, but the clock hands seem to split the quadrant evenly in half, meaning it must be six o'clock. Is he seriously calling her at six a.m. on Christmas morning to bitch about her still being asleep?

"Yesterday was snowing," Kate snaps, a little irritated. "No, these aren't excuses… Well, then I'll only enroll in the 10k, I'm fine with that, I don't need to shoot for a half-marathon."

Oh, so Mr. Sweaty Posts has probably been up since four-thirty, has already run twenty miles, and bench-pressed his way to Olympia. I roll my closed eyes. What a moron. I mean, fine, if that's what makes *you* happy then go for it, dude, but don't harass your girlfriend about not being as exercise-crazed as you are. Especially not on Christmas!

"I'm whispering because everyone else in the house is still asleep," Kate says. Another pause. "Yeah, okay, I'll call you later."

She drops the phone back on the nightstand with a loud thud, and then the mattress shifts as she presumably sags back on it.

I *could* pretend I'm still sleeping, but I can't help throwing a little dig in there. Flipping over, I rest my head on my elbow and say, "Ah, the joys of dating a morning person."

"Shut up, Chuck." She throws a pillow at my face.

I grab the pillow and stash it under my arm. "You're training for a half-marathon?"

"No," she says, with a bit too much emphasis. "I wish Marco would understand it's perfectly reasonable to pick up running without needing to run a marathon or compete in any race. Sometimes I just want to enjoy a simple jog with no pressure—the competition takes all the fun out of it. Also, it's normal to skip a day of training when it's snowing, or when I'm too tired from the night before!"

A smirk curls my lips as she finishes her rant. "No, I get it. I totally agree," I say. "Like how it's perfectly reasonable to visit a city without having to check *all* the boxes on the tourist guide and, you know, see the sights at a leisurely pace, no stress. No need to get up at the crack of dawn. And if it's pouring buckets outside, why not enjoy a cool beer and a burger in a cozy pub while listening to superb jazz music?"

I'm referring to the last trip Kate and I took together, to New Orleans. We argued endlessly about me being "too lazy" for not wanting to trudge around the city under the gushing rain, and for not appreciating being drawn into a streetcar ride made of soggy architecture, trees, and traffic that soaked up two hours of my life I'll never get back.

Mouth gaping, Kate glares at me and throws another pillow—her last.

I grab it and add it to my mound.

"I was never that pushy," she says.

"Really?" I raise an eyebrow. "Then I must've been dating a different Kate—Chuck-we-must-see-this-and-this-and-that—Warren for the past ten years."

She rolls her eyes. “Can I have my pillows back?”

“Sure,” I say, and playfully bash her with one, which prompts a straight-out pillow fight.

The match ends with Kate and I breathing hard, eyes locked. Before she can remind me again she has a boyfriend, I say, “Merry Christmas, Kate,” and whack her one more time. Then I run out of the room, yelling, “Last to sit at the kitchen table is a loser!”

Seventeen

Kate

Thanks to Marco's untimely wake-up call, Chuck and I are the first ones in the kitchen. It's honestly too early for anyone to be awake, but we get breakfast started anyway, because not even serving hot chocolate at one a.m. is enough to keep my family asleep for long on Christmas Day.

Chuck grabs plates and mugs from the cabinets and lays the table while I tune the stereo to the Christmas channel and then load the coffee maker while dancing along to *Jingle Bell Rock*. And I try really, really hard to ignore how cozy and familiar the arrangement feels. Or the confusing way my ex makes me feel these days. First, with all the talk of towels and sex, then with us having to kiss for the photo shoot, and this morning after that stupid pillow fight…

Truth is, I would've liked nothing more than to get rid of all the pillows and give the mattress's springs a real endurance test. Which is wrong for so many reasons. I don't even want to peek under that particular rug. And thankfully, I don't have to, at least not now.

As expected, the coffee has barely filled the pot when my parents both shuffle downstairs wearing matching robes from our bedroom line. Pops Teddy peeks in soon afterward, and the Roses break a record by arriving before eight-thirty—say what they might, I'm sure they've missed having their son under the same roof.

Breakfast is intentionally light, as Mom doesn't want to spoil anyone's appetite for the Christmas meal. And soon enough, we're ready to move outside for another Warren-

Rose tradition: our holiday interfamily snowman building competition. As sponsors of the official Bluewater Springs Annual Snow Sculpture Challenge, members of our families can't enter the contest, but we still like to host our own private competition in the backyard.

Nana and Pops have declined to take part for a few years now and have reserved for themselves the role of judges. To remain impartial, they're not allowed to know which team produced which sculpture until after they've announced the winners. Which leaves us with only three teams of two to sort. Not a business to be taken lightly, nonetheless.

We all gear up for the outdoors and Mom brings out the sacred black velvet sack containing our names carved on six wooden disks. Mom jostles the bag, and Bud is tasked with fishing out the names. We use the same method to decide teams for all our family games, from Christmas Pictionary to Charades to Family Feud.

Abigail is on my team, and the dads are together, which leaves Chuck with my mom. I don't envy him. Mom not only is a perfectionist, but she's also competitive and a sore loser. Whenever she loses, which, luckily, doesn't often happen, she blames whoever her unfortunate companion is. But with her craft mastery and Chuck's artistry, I'm sure they won't have any trouble winning this year.

I turn out to be right. We try to forfeit when we see how perfect Mom and Chuck's snow ballerina is, but Mom's a stickler for the rules, and she likes to have an awarding ceremony. Also, the losing team gets stuck doing the dishes tonight, so we need an official ranking. Abigail goes to summon the wise elders, who take a two-second look at the snow sculptures and declare Mom and Chuck's ballerina the winner. The snow snake that Abigail and I created gets us a nod and a smile from Pops and Nana, but even they can't make heads or tails of what the dads sculpted. A snow-dog, maybe, or a snow-bear? Something big and with four legs, for sure.

Unsurprisingly, the dads come in last. With nothing more to lose, Dad kneels and starts scraping together a snowball.

"Hooray for the winners." He stands and advances on Mom, tossing the snowball in the air and catching it, eyeing her suggestively.

"Mick Warren, you wouldn't dare," Mom says.

Dad throws the snowball, and Mom dodges behind her sculpture. The missile explodes against the ballerina, taking off one of her arms.

Mom and Chuck are outraged; they both pat together snowballs of their own, and all hell breaks loose. Snow projectiles fly in every direction and no one's safe. It's mayhem, a full-blown snowball fight. Chuck hits his dad square in the neck. Bud retaliates but catches Lillian instead. I'm so focused on sneaking up on Dad with an armful of snow that I don't even notice Mom's snowball until it hits me square in the shoulders.

Fifteen minutes after the fight starts, the snow sculptures are pulverized and the lawn that a couple of hours ago was a perfect, thick sheet of pristine white fluff is now reduced to a poultice of dirty snow. But everyone is laughing their heads off, and I suspect it will snow again soon to cover up our impromptu battlefield and restore the white blanketing.

We all stumble back into the house, shaking snow off our hair and clothes. When Dad removes his coat, an unexploded snowball that must've lodged in his collar splatters to the floor of the mudroom, and we all start laughing again.

Wet boots are exchanged for Chocolate Company slippers, and we all move into the living room to warm up by the fireplace. I'm exhausted but exhilarated.

The cheerful holiday spirit stays with me throughout the rest of the day. I don't even care that I'm not allowed any alcohol at lunch because of the fake baby. Nothing could dampen my good mood. Not even Josiane and her crew constantly flapping around the table with their cameras. Yes, they're a constant reminder of the Chucokate and the mess that awaits. But today Chuck and I took a vacation from the truth-telling business, so I'm going to enjoy Christmas and not think about all the wrong things in my life. And anyway, the camera crew takes off soon after the turkey is cut, leaving me completely free to live in the moment.

Half an hour later, I eat my last bite of turkey drowned in Mom's special cranberry sauce and recline in my chair, caressing my belly, contented. If not a real baby, I'm for sure carrying a food baby today.

My phone vibrates in my pocket. I check the screen: Marco. Still annoyed with him about this morning, I let the call go unanswered and fire him a quick text to tell him we're still eating and that I'll call him later.

I can't help but wonder how he—or any other boyfriend—would fit into this family picture.

No one will ever fit in as well as Chuck. Presently, my ex has an arm slung around Dad's shoulders, and they're half-drunkenly singing the University of Michigan Victors song.

As I watch them, another pang of regret sets in, a lump lodged in my throat that I find hard to swallow. Was breaking up with Chuck the right choice? This summer I felt like I had no choice, but just a few days home together and I'm questioning everything.

Luckily, Mom soon brings out the desserts, and the heavy chocolate content floods my system with handy endorphins that quickly push the wistfulness away. And so my good mood is restored just in time for the best part of the festivities. We leave our empty dishes behind—good luck with those, Dads—and gather around the Christmas tree to finally open the presents.

Like every year, it's a messy business of boxes switching hands, labels falling off, and gifts being opened by the wrong person and then returned to the legitimate owner.

I adore Christmas presents, and open mine with the same unabashed enthusiasm of when I was a little girl. This year I've collected a moisturizer facial cream set, a copy of *What to Expect When You're Expecting*, new snow boots, and the usual fifty bucks from Pops. Except for Pops' gift, which has been the same for as long as I can remember, I'm not sure who gave me what. As expected, most of the labels fell off beforehand or got stuck to the wrong package. But to guess and be wrong and find out later is part of the fun.

Lastly, I open a tiny square box and squeal in excitement when I discover a fitness watch. I might not want to run a half-marathon, but I've enjoyed tracking my progress on the app Marco downloaded for me. And I have to admit, I relish the morale boost that comes from earning all those achievements badges.

I stare up at the crowd, shaking the watch. "Who is this from? I love it!"

From the other side of the room, Chuck stares up at me and I immediately know the watch is from him. And if I already had it on my wrist, those cardio-zone minutes would pile up like greased lightning considering how fast my pulse is racing.

And before I can process my gut's reaction, I panic once more, because I've just realized something. Holding Chuck's gaze, I blurt out, "I forgot your present."

Eighteen

Chuck

I stare at Kate's legitimately sorrowful eyes and all I want to do is get her out of the tough spot. In our family, she's considered the master gifter, who always picks a personal and thoughtful gift for everyone, and now everyone's staring at her in confused silence. They probably didn't think she could forget a present. And when she says she forgot me, I know what she really means is that she didn't buy me anything because she didn't imagine she'd have to give me a present this year. Back in Ann Arbor, we both assumed that by Christmas our separation would be official.

As the room is held in a suspenseful silence, I realize this would be the perfect occasion to confess the truth. That Kate dumped me, that the engagement and the baby are fake, and that she's dating a gym stud who's obsessed with health apps, running stats, and who probably counts calories when he eats.

But as a worried shadow crosses Nana Fern's face, I can't bring myself to speak up. I know Kate and I are only digging a deeper grave every day we delay the inevitable, but the more we lie, the more it seems impossible to stop. Our lies are hurting us, but telling the truth will hurt everyone else. There must be a way we can get out of this with no one's heart getting broken.

Except for mine, of course, but that ship sailed a long time ago.

With all eyes still on us, I spin Kate's admission with humor. Laughing like I don't have a care in the world, I say teasingly, "Next time I tell you to pack only the essential, you should listen to me." I chuckle nervously. "With everything that I had to stuff in the car, I'm surprised we didn't leave behind more."

Everyone chuckles along. Kate half-grimaces, half-smiles at my save—a new expression she's been perfecting since we came home—and follows my lead. "Well, that's what you get for trying to find your present before Christmas. I must have hidden it so well I completely forgot about it."

Lillian jumps in. "Don't worry, Honeybun, it's perfectly normal to become a little forgetful when you're expecting. You must already have pregnancy brain."

Kate stares at her mom. "Pregnancy brain?"

"Oh, yes, Darling," my mom piles on. "Say goodbye to your wits for the next three years, and just wait until those hormones really kick in! You're going to lose it completely. All the info is in the book." She points at her present for Kate.

"But all the suffering will be worth it once you hug your baby for the first time," Lillian says, mimicking cuddling a newborn in her arms.

Everyone coos over the imaginary baby. At least they've forgotten about my missing present.

***

When all the gifts have been unwrapped, we settle down to watch the traditional Christmas afternoon family movie—*Godmothered* is the choice for this year. Once the movie's over, my parents distribute a round of hugs and then head home, while Kate and I retire upstairs.

"What a day," I say, blowing hair away from my forehead.

"Right." Kate sighs as she sits on the bed. "You know, for

a minute there I thought you were going to spill the beans."

I sit next to her. "I considered it, but the concerned expression on Nana Fern's face made me cop out. Would you have wanted me to speak up?"

Kate studies me for a long moment, then shakes her head. "No, Chuck, you were right to keep quiet. It was… nice. To have one last Christmas together."

My chest tightens as I try to picture the holidays with the Warrens and the Roses not under the same roof. I can't even remember a Christmas not spent with them—not spent with Kate. What will it be like next year? Will Christmas Day still be a joint celebration, but with Kate and me bringing different dates? The idea of spending the holidays with Marco the Ripped is nauseating.

***

I don't sleep very well that night, and neither does Kate. She tosses and turns next to me, and I couldn't honestly say who falls asleep first. When I do manage to sleep, anxious nightmares haunt me—of us telling our parents the truth, of Nana Fern having a fainting spell, of The Bluewater Springs Chocolate Company going under, all because of us…

When I wake up, acid is burning in my stomach. I take the usual squint at my wristwatch: six a.m. Even though Marco hasn't called today to check on Kate's shaky resolve to go for a run in the dead of winter, a few days of his early calls have been enough to align my biorhythm to his absurd schedule.

I turn my head on the pillow and find Kate equally awake, staring at the ceiling.

"Didn't get much sleep, uh?" I say.

"Nope." She huffs a bout of air out of her mouth.

"Today's the day we tell them."

"Mm-hm."

"Nervous?"

She turns to me. "Worse than when we had to confess we'd eaten all of Mrs. Potter's cherries straight off the tree."

I laugh, remembering our incursion on the Potters' farm as fifth graders. The fruit heist wouldn't have been so egregious on its own. Our parents could've paid Mrs. Potter back for the stolen products and we could've gotten off with a minor grounding. Except, we had picked clean Mrs. Potter's precious Autumn Flowering Cherry tree, which she had been nurturing with extra special care. She talked to the damn tree every day, trying to bribe it into producing its best cherries that she planned to enter in the Cherry Blossom Festival Best Cherry Competition.

Once the cherries theft was discovered, the town basked in the infamous whodunit mystery for an entire afternoon. Until both Kate and I got sick from having eaten too many cherries and got caught. As punishment, our parents made us work on the Potters' farm for free all summer.

Worst summer of our lives. Mrs. Potter was a devil of a vindictive old woman.

I laugh. "Do you suppose they're going to banish us to a farm again?"

Kate chuckles. "Honestly, that wouldn't be the worst thing."

"But we agree, we tell them today?"

Kate nods. "This morning, after breakfast."

I text Mom and ask them to come over to the Warrens' house as soon as they can. They arrive at around ten with Nana Fern in tow. We assemble the parents and grandparents in the living room and, holding hands for strength and moral support, we launch into our half-rehearsed speech.

"Thank you all for being here," Kate says. "I know these last few days have been a whirlwind, but Chuck and I need to tell you that—"

"You're having twins?" Lillian interrupts.

Kate's mouth dangles open in disbelief. "No, Mom, we're not having twins! In fact, quite the opposite."

This time my mom interrupts. "Oh my gosh, is something wrong with the baby?"

"No, Mom," I say. "There's nothing wrong with the baby, because there's no—"

The Warrens' obnoxiously loud doorbell rings, filling the house with the tune of a thousand bells and preventing everyone in the room from hearing the end of my speech confessing there's no baby.

Mick stands up. "Excuse me for a second," he says, and goes to answer the door.

Loud, cheerful greetings are exchanged, and Mick walks back into the living room followed by Kate's aunt and uncle.

The newcomers are jointly carrying an extravagantly large present. A belated Christmas gift, perhaps?

Unfortunately, Mick's introduction is much more disturbing. "Uncle Jo and Aunt Mary have brought you kids an early wedding gift!"

Kate and I exchange a desperate look. Aunt Mary is one of the worst gossips in town; we can't announce our breakup now that she's here. So, we thank them, invite them to stay for a hot chocolate, and sit down for a good thirty minutes of nastily dull small talk.

We've barely got rid of Uncle Jo and Aunt Mary when the doorbell rings again. This time our unexpected guests are the Baxters. The husband, Carl, was the first employee of

The Bluewater Springs Chocolate Company, and even if he's retired now, he's still a family friend. He comes in with his wife to bring us yet another wedding gift. And the dance starts all over again. Bluewater Springs Insta Chocolate Mix is brewed, served, and sprinkled in small talk.

The procession of gift bearers continues all day. It's as if the entire town picked today to bring us their wedding presents and arranged their visits on a tight schedule. Considering how Bluewater Springs works, they probably did conspire. Or, more likely, someone said they'd deliver their gift today and the others, not to be outdone, followed suit.

A few visitors stay over for lunch, and the social calls don't stop throughout the afternoon.

By the time we've thanked and small-talked all the guests, my cheeks ache from all the fake smiling. And after stashing all the gifts in Kate's room, we're both too mentally and physically exhausted to tackle any serious grand discourse with our families.

We sag on the bed and stare at each other.

"Do you think we'll have to return all these gifts after we cancel the wedding?" I ask.

"I'll marry you just to not have to see all those people again." Kate groans.

"No, seriously, how did they buy presents so quickly?"

"And with all the shops being closed yesterday, too." Kate suddenly gasps.

"What?"

"I just realized all our wedding presents will probably be horrible, recycled Christmas gifts with different wrapping paper."

"Good," I say.

"Why is that good?"

"Because no one will want ugly, recycled Christmas presents returned."

"Oh." Kate turns on her side to look at me. "Chuck, do you think the universe is trying to send us a message here?"

"What message?"

"That it doesn't want our parents to learn the truth." She leans back and sighs. "Maybe we should just stop fighting it, get married, and be done with it."

My guard is down and, in a moment of excessive sincerity, I blurt, "I don't want to marry you that way."

Kate's eyes become huge… because I've basically just told her I want to marry her.

But before she can reply, the doorbell chimes again, and we both groan in actual physical pain at the idea of having to repeat the dance one more time.

Then Lillian's voice drifts up the stairs. "Kate, it's a friend of yours."

"We'll be down in a second, Mom."

"Okay," Lillian shout's back. "I'll make Marco a hot chocolate in the meantime."

Marco!

The name registers in both our minds at the same time, and we turn to each other, hands on our faces, mouths open in a silent scream a la Macaulay Culkin in *Home Alone.*

Nineteen

Kate

I rush down the stairs, Chuck following closely on my heels. We careen into the kitchen and find Marco seated at the island on a stool, his coat unbuttoned but still on, a military-green rucksack dropped at his feet.

"Marco," I say, straining so much to smile my lips might crack.

He turns, stands up, and hugs me, going for a kiss full on the mouth. I turn my face at the last minute and his lips land on my cheek. I quickly push him away, and Chuck rushes in to hug him and pat his back, saying, "You made it, man. So glad you could come."

Marco blinks at Chuck, bewildered, and is thankfully too shocked to react. He knows who Chuck is, but they've never met face to face; my ex-boyfriend is probably the last person Marco expected to find at my house.

Mom, who up until a second ago was frowning at Marco's handling of me, relaxes and smiles at the knowledge he's supposedly Chuck's dear friend. "I was making Marco a hot chocolate." She turns toward the stove and grabs a clean mug. "Are you here for the wedding, Marco? Kate, Chuck, if you have other guests coming in from Ann Arbor you should tell me; I'm already working on the seating arrangements, and the Beach Club has limited space."

Marco frowns. "What wed—"

Before he can complete the phrase, I slap my hand over his mouth and grab his elbow. "You know, Mom, we've had enough hot chocolate for today. We're going for a beer in town. See you later."

And before she can reply, or Marco can protest, we've dragged him into the hall and are putting on our coats and snow boots.

As soon as we step outside, Marco wheels on me. "What's going on here? What wedding? Why are you two together?"

"Not here," I say, and pull him down the driveway. He follows, albeit grumbling the whole way. Chuck wisely keeps his mouth shut and lets me handle it.

We walk for about ten minutes in strained silence and stop at a small park about half a mile from my parents' house. In the rush of getting away, I forgot to put on gloves, and my fingers are already going numb. I jam my hands in my pockets to warm them, and pace around as I tell Marco everything that has happened in the last few days, trying not to sound too crazy. Chuck looms in the background a few feet away from us silently observing.

"You mean you've been lying to me, all this time?" Marco says when I'm finished.

"Technically, yes, but only because the timing didn't matter, what difference do a few days make?"

"Let's see," Marco says, mock pensive. "Only that if you keep postponing, you'll end up married!" He points his finger between me and Chuck. "I still can't believe he proposed, and you said yes!"

"I told you it was a complete misunderstanding."

From the distance, Chuck shouts, "Totally unintentional, dude."

"You stay out of this!" Marco snaps.

"Or what?" Chuck says, and then, under his breath, adds, "What're you gonna do, bench press me?"

"What did you just say to me?"

"Nothing." Chuck again follows up with a whispered provocation. "Idiot."

"*Cabrón,*" Marco retorts.

"Jerk."

"*Pendecho.*"

The last thing I need right now is for my fake fiancé and my real boyfriend to get into a fight.

"Listen," I say, grabbing Marco by the shoulders and guiding him a little further away. "Please bear with me, just for tonight. Now is too late to talk to our families, and we're all tired, and Chuck's parents aren't at the house anyway. But I promise we will tell them tomorrow morning first thing. No excuses this time."

"And what about tonight?" Marco asks. "Where am I supposed to sleep?"

That's a good question. We have a guest bedroom in the house in theory but it's so filled up with Mom's paraphernalia it's a hazard to even enter. "You can crash in the barn," I say.

Keeping him and Chuck under two separate roofs might not be a bad idea as well.

Marco doesn't agree.

"While *he* sleeps in your room?" he protests.

"It's totally innocent, you know that. I broke up with *him*, remember?"

Chuck's face falls at that, but he'll have to suck it up, because Marco's my priority right now. And Marco clearly isn't happy about the sleeping arrangements, but after a little more convincing he finally comes 'round.

As we start to head back home, Chuck accidentally-on-purpose bumps shoulders with Marco. "By the way," he says, marching on and kicking at chunks of ice the snowplow has amassed by the side of the road. "If anyone asks, you have a girlfriend."

"I *do* have a girlfriend."

Chuck replies without turning or stopping. "Well, in this town it's not Kate."

And just when I thought things couldn't get any worse… When it rains, it pours.

Twenty

Chuck

That night, Kate tries to sneak out of the house to join Sweaty Posts in the barn at least three times, but she gets caught every single time.

On the first two attempts, bad luck tromps her as she bumps into her parents wandering around the house for their own mysterious reasons. Maybe they're hoping to overhear more inaccurate details of our personal lives.

On the third try—which she waits until past midnight to pull off—she gets sloppy. As she walks down the stairs, she forgets to skip the third-to-last step, which always creaks—rookie mistake—and wakes up Pops Teddy, who sleeps on the first floor and has ears as sharp as a bat. He also claims to keep alert even while sleeping: a legacy of the Vietnam War, according to him.

From the bed, I listen as he asks his granddaughter what she's doing sneaking around the house so late.

Kate replies she got thirsty. A long silence follows, then the sound of the fridge opening, closing, and finally her muffled steps climbing back up the stairs in trudging defeat.

"Are you giving up on your romantic rendezvous anytime soon?" I ask as she slumps into the room. "I'd like to sleep, and you keep waking me up."

"Don't worry, Chuck," she snaps back. "Tomorrow night you'll be in your room alone and no one will disturb you ever again."

That shuts me up all right. I turn on my side and brood in silence. Kate slips under the covers next to me, equally unhappy. She doesn't move or make any sound, but I can tell she's moping. It takes us forever to fall asleep again.

When Kate's alarm goes off at six o'clock the next morning, I'm ready to murder someone. A very specific tan-skinned, rip-chested, fitness-maniac dude.

Ah, now that the half-marathon police has arrived in town, Kate is suddenly all aboard the early-morning-run train. She's up and dressed well before sunrise and takes off into the polar temperatures with her muscle-head boyfriend for an hour-long jogging session.

When Kate gets back, I'm still nestled under the covers and don't plan to get up anytime soon.

But I don't have a choice. Once Kate has showered and changed, she marches over and yanks the comforter off me.

"You need to pack," she tells me.

"Relax," I say, trying to grab the covers and warmth back. "What's the hurry? My parents won't arrive before ten anyway."

"It doesn't matter. I want you out of my room."

"You, or Marco?"

Kate's face crumbles. "I'm sorry, Chuck. I know I'm being a bitch for no reason. But with Marco coming here… Gosh, that was the *last* thing I needed. As if I wasn't stressed enough already. I'm doing the best I can."

I don't doubt the professor has been giving her an earful for every extra second she unnecessarily spends in my presence. Taking pity on her, I get up with a shrug. "Don't worry, I've heard fake-pregnant women get short-tempered all the time."

That wrestles a smile out of her. "That must be it. Thank you, Chuck, really for being so understanding…"

It looks like she wants to say more, but she doesn't.

"Give me a moment to get dressed and grab my stuff," I say. "I'll meet you downstairs."

By the time breakfast is over, it's past nine-thirty and I'm so sick and tired of Marco's glares that I've become as eager as Kate to get down to business and finally come clean with our parents.

"Lillian," I say. "Do you know when my mom and dad plan to arrive? Kate and I would like to talk to you all."

With the sweetest smile, Lillian replies, "Oh, they're not coming here this morning. We're meeting them somewhere else."

"Where?" I ask.

"I can't say." Lillian makes a zipping-my-mouth gesture. "But we're going on a field trip. It's a surprise."

I throw a worried glance at Kate and read the same terror in her eyes. This can't be good.

"But, Mom, I was—" Kate pauses, then starts again. "I mean, *Chuck* and I were planning to show Marco around town today. Can't we do the field trip tomorrow?"

"No, Honeybun, we made plans." Then, turning to Sweaty Posts, she adds, "Marco, you're welcome to tag along, of course. And once we're done there, Chuck and Kate can show you around town all they want." She checks her watch. "We could even make it back in time for you to join the noon tour at the factory. Bernie is handling that, and he's our best guide—except for Chuck and Kate, of course."

I like how Marco isn't able to come up with any objections and promptly gets rolled under the Warren-Rose overbearing parenting style just a few hours after having joined the club.

***

With six of us now going on this mystery field trip—Pops Teddy is coming, too—we have to take two cars. I refuse to go anywhere near Marco's ridiculous red sports BMW, so I go outside a few minutes early to free the Versa from the snow. Despite the shining sun, the air is frigid, which makes scraping the windshield particularly hard. To make a half-decent job, I have to turn on the car to get a little help from the interior heating. I've done half the windshield when Sweaty Posts comes out of the barn.

"We could've gone in my car," he says. "I have a heated windshield."

Of course he does.

The BMW, having arrived only yesterday, isn't as snowed in as the Versa, but I'd rather scrape a thousand frozen-solid cars than catch a ride with Marco. And with him driving, I'd probably get carsick in two seconds. And while throwing up in Marco's sports car would be thrilling, I prefer not to show any weaknesses before the enemy.

"It's okay," I say. "I'm almost done, anyway."

Mick and Lillian come out a few minutes later, followed by Kate and Pops Teddy. She's helping him walk down the driveway, making sure he doesn't slip on the ice.

Once Kate has safely delivered Pops Teddy to her father's SUV, she joins Marco and me next to the Nissan. Then she pauses, and turns to yell at her mother, "Where is it we're going again?"

"Don't worry, Honeybun, just follow us."

Lillian climbs into their car, and we pile into the rental.

No matter how much pre-heating I did, it still takes a good ten minutes before the temperature in the Nissan becomes acceptable. Especially since we're driving as fast as a sedated slug. Mick insisted on driving and is keeping a good five miles under the speed limit, even in twenty-five mile an hour zones, and, given the overnight freeze, he's proceeding with even more caution than usual. I swear, in a previous life he must've been a DMV instructor or a traffic enforcer.

We drive out of town for about fifteen minutes along the coast until Mick lights the blinker and turns to the right. We pass through a perfectly pristine white picket fence that marks the beginning of a neat cobblestone driveway. A wooden signpost identifies the place as Sunrise House.

Kate's dad parks next to my parents' car which is already lined up next to another car in front of a huge house with light-blue wood siding that overlooks Lake Michigan.

I pull up on the other side, and we all get out of our respective cars and go through the usual rounds of greetings, kisses, and hugs. At least, until my mom spots Marco, does a double-take, and asks, "And who's this handsome young man?"

I roll my eyes. Thank you, Mom, for pointing out the obvious.

Lillian, enjoying being more informed on what's going on with the "younger crowds," takes it upon herself to make the introductions.

"This is Marco Guerra. He's a good friend of Chuck and Kate's. They've invited him to the wedding!"

Mom, who until that last phrase had been ogling the beef cake, turns toward me and asks, "Really? Is he in the wedding party?"

"No, Mom," I say. "Only Phil, Gary, and Finn are. Since Kate has three bridesmaids, we wanted to keep things even."

Lillian jumps back in at this point. "You have three bridesmaids, Honeybun? I thought you only wanted cousin Gretchen."

"Gretchen is my maid of honor, Mom. I'm going to need bridesmaids as well," Kate says, as if this is something we've discussed plenty of times in the past.

Lying has become such second nature to us, I'm afraid by the end of this holiday we both will have trouble remembering what's real and what isn't. Marco's angry frown at this casual discussion of wedding arrangements is an excellent reality check, though.

The wedding talk gets mercifully interrupted by a woman in a business suit exiting the house. She rushes down the front steps, waving in greeting. "Ah, everyone's here, how marvelous. Shall we go in?"

Between us, the parents, the grandparents—Nana Fern tagged along, too—and Marco, we take a while to squeeze through the entrance door and reassemble inside.

"As you can see, the first floor is one big open space," the woman says. "And light pours in from the wall-wide windows at the back. And I probably shouldn't reveal the showstopper right away, but what can I say? I like to start every visit with a bang. Please come this way."

She heads to the French doors, and I dutifully follow, even if I don't understand why our parents have arranged a visit to a house in the middle of nowhere. Are they planning to expand our office facilities? Why would they buy space so far from the factory?

Then I get excited. Is this going to be a detached think-tank reserved for the creative team? That would actually make total sense. I could see myself working here, where the light is so much better than in my tiny office back at the factory—incidentally, what used to be my old bedroom. Oh yes, this is definitely a change I could get behind.

The real estate agent swings open the French doors and

walks out onto the deck. “Admire. The property is endowed with far-reaching bay views and over a thousand feet of shared waterfront.” She swipes her arm toward the shore. “We’re a little past sunrise now, but I can assure you the view at dawn is a staggering watercolor marvel that will greet your every morning. And at night, the absolute peace and tranquility will make the perfect backdrop for entertaining evening guests.”

Evening guests? Isn’t that a weird feature for a new office? Unless our parents mean to turn this into some kind of showroom. Or she’s gotten her clients mixed up and thinks we want to live here.

“Of course,” the real estate agent continues, “this is only the first of three large cedar decks, and the house also features a flagstone patio that wraps along the back on that side. Do you like the view?” This question is directed at me, solidifying my theory that the house is meant to become our new creative headquarters.

I stare out at the frozen-over lake, snow-covered lawn, and tall fig trees. The landscape is stunning, and the agent knows it. I tell her as much.

Pleased with the answer, she escorts us back inside. “The kitchen has a beautiful island and is a proper cook’s kitchen with top-of-the-line appliances.”

Makes sense. Maybe Lillian is tired of using her own kitchen to do all the creative experiments, and she and Dad want to secure an additional space where they can express all their culinary genius. I like the vibe of this house. It has a ton of potential.

“The first floor also has a full bath, laundry, and library,” the agent continues. “Shall we move upstairs?”

We all follow, except for the elderly who opt to sit on the

veranda to enjoy the views. Once they're safely settled in their Adirondack chairs, and they've assured us they won't try to wander off on their own and break a hip, we move on to the second floor.

"The upper level boasts five bedrooms, three baths, and the master suite. Let's start with the smaller room first. It would be perfect for a nursery."

A… nursery? That's a little odd in an office, but our parents might plan to offer a childcare service as a benefit for employees with children? To be Socially Responsible is becoming more and more important for companies, and we've been named among Michigan's top employers five years in a row. Guess they don't want to let go of the title.

When we reach the last room, the real estate agent becomes even more ecstatic. "See the master? How huge the room is, and it features a private Jack-and-Jill bath and his-and-hers walk-in closets. Take as much time as you need to peek around," she concludes. "I'm going to wait for you downstairs."

It's a gorgeous master suite, for sure. Again, not sure how useful it'll be when we turn this place into the Creative Department's headquarters. Maybe it could become my office? Turn the walk-in closets into storage rooms? I suppose I could see that working…

When we all reassemble downstairs around the kitchen island, our parents look as excited as the real estate agent.

"What do you think?" they ask me and Kate.

"It's beautiful," Kate says. I nod in agreement. "But why exactly are we looking at a new house? Are you guys moving?"

Oh, it never occurred to me Kate's parents might've been looking at the house for themselves.

"Not us," Lillian says. "The house is your wedding present. We bought it for you. Surprise!"

My stomach drops and, not having a mirror, I can't say whose face looks worse at this announcement: mine, Kate's, or Marco's.

Twenty-one

Kate

Marco displays an uncharacteristic amount of patience by waiting until we're back at the house and out of my parents' earshot to lay into me about this latest debacle.

"You have to tell them, Kate," he says. "Do you know how hard it was to keep my mouth shut back there? When they said the house was a wedding present, I wanted to punch a hole through the wall!"

I pull the barn door open and usher him inside. "I know, I know. They blindsided me, too, you know?"

"What happened to telling them everything? You promised."

"But did you see how excited my parents were about the new house?" I sigh as I sit by the antique fireplace and start nibbling on a cuticle. "How could we tell them after that?"

"Kate, come on, you know this has gone too far." Marco sits next to me. "Your parents just bought you a *mansion.* They're convinced you're getting married on Friday. The more time you wait, the more lies pile on, and the harder it'll get to tell the truth."

"Don't you think I know that?" I grab a fire poker and stab at the ashes, just to have something to do with my hands. "It just never seems to be the right time. What was I supposed to do, blurt out the truth in front of the real estate agent?"

"The wedding's in four days. You're running out of 'the right time.'"

"I'll tell them tomorrow."

"You said that yesterday."

"Well, I didn't expect the house."

"Always an excuse."

"Not this time. Tomorrow we'll tell them."

Marco removes the fire poker from my hands and holds them in his. "You promise?"

"I promise."

***

Marco's mood doesn't improve when I tell him I have to go to that stupid premarital counseling session with Chuck this afternoon. My boyfriend stays close to mute throughout lunch and excuses himself as soon as the meal is over. I can't go after him without arousing too many suspicions, I can only watch him through the dining room window as he exits the barn in his sporty gear and goes for a jog in the freezing outdoors. No matter that we already ran this morning, exercise is how he copes with things.

Besides, he always feels better after a run. Endorphins, in thee I trust to save my relationship.

To get to church on time, Chuck and I have to leave before Marco is back. And at two-thirty on the dot, we walk into Pastor Grant's office, ready for a two-hour lecture on how to make our relationship work through the highs and lows of married life. Maybe we should've taken this class a few years ago, back when our love story was still salvageable.

The pastor welcomes us with a warm smile. "Chuck, Kate, perfect timing."

Instead of inviting us to sit on the chairs before his desk, the pastor gets up, picks up his jacket from the backrest of his chair, and beckons us out of the office. "Please come this way. I like to hold my premarital courses in a different room."

We dutifully follow him down a long, narrow corridor until we reach the designated room. The space isn't large, but it's cozy. Carpeted floor, colorful pillows scattered all over, and a red chenille ball resting in the middle. No chairs, I notice.

"Please take off your shoes," Pastor Grant asks us, doing the same.

We do as we're told and follow him inside.

"Sit wherever you like. On a pillow, grab one to hold, whatever makes you comfortable."

Chuck clears his throat. "Should we just sit on the floor?"

"Yes," Pastor Grant confirms. "In my many years of counseling, I've found a less formal environment fosters more honest conversations."

We all sit on the carpet, forming a small, three-person circle. Instinctively, I grab a big, fluffy pillow and place it over my crossed legs, hugging it to my chest.

"Very well." Pastor Grant launches into a speech about what being married means, and how much hard work couples need to pour into a relationship to make it function. Blah blah blah. I try not to tune him out, but really, it's not like this advice actually applies to us. I sneak a glance at Chuck; he looks like he's about to fall asleep on the pillow tucked beside him.

After the introductory sermon is over, the pastor progresses to explain how the session will be structured. "Usually, I discuss various topics with my couples, like how well they know each other, or if they share the same views on starting a family." He stares pointedly at my belly. "But I assume it's safe to skip both with you. Instead, the principal topic I wanted to tackle today is conflict. How to avoid it, and when an argument inevitably occurs, how to deal with it constructively. These discussions can, from time to time, get heated, so the only rule I have is that we don't talk over each other."

Pastor Grant grabs the red chenille ball. "This"—he rotates the soft ball in his hand—"is the talking ball. Only the person holding it is allowed to speak. Everything clear so far?"

We nod.

"Very well. So, conflict. You've been together a long time; how do you cope with arguments? Kate, ladies first."

He hands me the ball, putting me on the spot whether I like it or not.

I hold the ball on top of the pillow in my lap and ponder for a second. Chuck and I never fought much, mostly because he was too passive to argue. I try to remember a big fight or something, but I can't. And since we're not really here to discuss our non-existent relationship, I might as well chalk out whatever answer and be done with the discussion.

"We're cool," I say. "We never argue that much, anyway."

I give the ball back to Pastor Grant.

"Okay," he says, and turns to my fake fiancé. "Chuck, let's hear from you. How do you handle conflict as a couple?"

Chuck takes the talking ball, and I expect him to follow my lead and confirm we're awesome at handling conflict. Anything to make this counseling session end faster. Instead, staring down at the ball, he says, "Kate is very passive-aggressive, Pastor. Whenever something bothers her, she doesn't outright say it. She gets sulky and makes all these subtle comments, expecting me to divine what she's mad about. And when I don't read her mind, she gets even madder on the inside, but quieter on the outside. If I ask her what's wrong, she repeats 'nothing' a million times, and then a week, a month, a year later she explodes at me with all the stuff she's been keeping bottled up."

WHOA. WHOA. WHOA. Where did this Kate-is-the-passive-aggressive-queen nonsense come from?

"That's not true," I protest.

Pastor Grant raises a hand. "Kate, please, Chuck has the talking ball. Let him finish. Anything else you'd like to add, Chuck?"

"Yeah, she's touchy. And if I point it out, she gets offended and even more passive-aggressive."

Chuck hands the ball back, and Pastor Grant passes it to me. I snatch it from his hands, ready to mount my defense. "Nothing of what he said is true. I'm not passive-aggressive, and I can take constructive criticism like a mature adult."

"Is that all you have to say, Kate?" Pastor Grant asks.

"Yes."

"Because right now you look pretty offended. Are you sure nothing of what Chuck said is true?" Then, turning to that treacherous ijit, the pastor adds, "Chuck, can you give an example of an occasion on which Kate has been passive-aggressive or not forthcoming about something that upset her?"

Chuck stares at me, evidently waiting for the ball, so he can spew more falsehoods. I throw it at him, and he barely catches it. And I'm aware my actions are proving him right, but he made me furious. Where does he get off, throwing false accusations at me? Especially since we aren't together anymore. What's the point? Is he trying to humiliate me? Is this revenge for the breakup? Or is Chuck mad because

Marco's here, and he's taking it out on me? This morning I thought he was being really mature about the situation; I didn't expect such a low blow.

Chuck cradles the ball in his hands for a while before he talks. "Like… take the dishes. One evening, I didn't do them right after dinner when it was my turn because of a special on TV I wanted to watch live."

I remember that night. Chuck spent it slumped on the couch watching a two-hour documentary on Dungeons and Dragons.

"I left the dishes in the sink to deal with later. But she decided that meant I wasn't going to clean up ever and started making weird comments about how we live in a world with supposed gender equality but the women are still expected to do most of the housework. Then she got up, did the dishes in my place, and went to bed fuming."

"You know I hate waking up to a dirty kitchen," I interrupt. "And you didn't even say thank you I washed up in your place." For once, Pastor Grant doesn't reprimand me for having spoken without the precious talking ball.

"I forgot, Kate, okay? Because dishes are not that big of a deal for me. If I'd seen them in the sink, I would've loaded the dishwasher. End of story."

"No, you would have forgotten about them and let them sit there rotting for days, just like you always do."

"That's not—!"

"Chuck," Pastor Grant interrupts. "How do you know Kate was mad about the dishes, if Kate didn't tell you that evening and you forgot the issue completely?"

"She threw it all back at me a few months ago when she bro—" Chuck hastily cuts himself off. "I mean, we had a huge argument a while back, and she complained about a lot of things I didn't even know were an issue."

"Like the dishes?"

"Among other things."

"Such as?"

Chuck blushes from neck to ears. "Nothing important."

"This is a safe space, Chuck. We can't make any progress if you don't speak honestly."

Chuck shoots a panicked glance my way. I ignore him. He dug this hole; he can get himself out of it.

"Like, um…" Chuck stammers. "Well, she thought I was no longer interested in… uh… being intimate with her. And instead of confronting me, she pulled some absurd internet towel test on me that I didn't even know was a thing."

Oh. My. Gosh. He *DID NOT* just mention the towel test in front of a pastor!

"Maybe I wouldn't have had to resort to a dumb test if you'd spent more than two minutes away from your PlayStation," I retort.

"It's always the PlayStation with you!" Chuck shouts. "Don't you think I'd burn that damn thing to ashes, along with every video game I've ever owned, if I thought it would fix what happened?"

He's panting, and his eyes are blazing with intensity, and… I stare back, utterly confused once again. Where did all this passion come from? And why didn't he tell me all these things when we broke up, he barely put up a fight, I assumed he was okay with the decision. But now…

This premarital session is scrambling my already muddled feelings even more.

Pastor Grant blinks at us. "Could fix what, Chuck? What happened between you two?"

Chuck stares at the pastor in shock, as if suddenly

realizing a third person is in the room.

"Nothing," he says. "I just… never realized video games were such a thorn in her side. I wish she'd told me."

"I didn't think I had to," I say. It was so obvious. To me, anyway. Did he really not get that?

"Kate." Pastor Grant stares at me. "Do you think you could be more assertive in expressing what you want out of your relationship with Chuck?"

"I can try," I say. "But Chuck could work on that, too,"

"Can you elaborate, Kate?"

While formally answering Pastor Grant's question, I stare at Chuck. "He didn't tell me any of these things when we had our big argument four months ago. If he had…"

I trail off.

Chuck's eyes are still blazing with passion as he stares at me intently. "You're saying it could have gone differently if I'd said something?"

"I don't know, Chuck. Maybe?"

"Maybe," he repeats, like he's turning the word over and over in his head. Then he adds, "I should have said something."

"Yeah, you should have."

"This is substantial progress…" Pastor Grant says, but I don't pay attention to whatever rambling sermon he launches into. I'm lost looking at Chuck, struggling to figure out what's going through his head.

The way he talks, he sounds like someone who'd do anything to turn back time.

Why?

Is he still in love with me?

And why is that possibility making my head spin?

Twenty-two

Chuck

Today is the day. No more excuses.

I wake up ready for battle.

With Marco in Bluewater Springs, the lie Kate and I have been carrying around has become too heavy. I can't stand it when she comes to bed with his sickening cologne all over her. Even if I'm sure they haven't had a chance to have sex since he arrived, seeing them together is still unbearable.

Time to put an end to the farce.

I pull on a pair of jeans and a branded Chocolate Company sweater with a gingerbread man—I try never to lose my humor, even when facing the firing squad—and head down to breakfast.

Kate, of course, has already been up for hours, ran at least ten miles, and showered. Ever since we got back from our session with Pastor Grant yesterday, she's been doing her best to avoid me. Because of Marco, or because of what we said at the session? Before his surprise visit, we were returning to our old selves. But now the truce is over. My sweet, fun Kate has been replaced by training-for-half-a-marathon, suddenly-concerned-about-the-economic-state-of-the-country Kate. Listening to Marco make conversation at the dinner table and watching Kate agree with every boring, unoriginal banality he says is driving me crazy.

It kills me to see how hard she works to impress Marco. She shouldn't. Marco should already be impressed, because Kate is perfect just the way she is.

And now that I've started thinking in Bruno Mars' lyrics,

I should slap myself, get my act together, and finish this charade once and for all.

I take the stairs two at a time and, once on the first floor, skid to the kitchen's threshold. Marco and Kate are already seated at the island, displaying twin morose expressions.

Lillian is hopping between the stoves singing Christmas tunes under her breath while she puts the final touches on whatever she's making, oblivious to the silent fight that's taking place behind her back.

The tension between Kate and Marco is so thick I could cut it with a knife. Sullen and quiet, they're sitting next to each other but leaning in opposites directions, as if to establish a little distance between themselves.

Um, trouble in paradise? My heart soars… and then drops equally fast when I notice they're not just glaring at empty space—they both keep throwing dirty looks at the back corner of the kitchen.

Since I can't see what they're scowling at, I step into the room and take a stool opposite Kate's. My ex glowers at me, too. What did I do? I just got here.

Then I throw a quick glance at the now-visible corner of the kitchen, and the reason for her bad mood becomes clear. Hidden under the infamous burgundy veil is another lumpy shape that looks worryingly humanoid.

Dread fills me as I déjà vu to our first night home and the unveiling of the Chucokate. What have our parents concocted this time?

I clear my throat. "Err, Lillian, I see we have another unveiling planned. Is it a new surprise?"

Lillian turns around. "Oh, Chuck, good morning. I didn't see you come in. And I already told Kate, no spoilers, you must wait until your parents arrive. Ah, you kids are really two peas in a pod, always asking the same questions."

Lillian's declaration produces a wave of winces around the table. She doesn't notice, as she's already returned to her cooking. Which is some sort of... broth? It smells funny. What on Earth is she making?

Kate glares at me even harder.

What does she expect me to do, magic away whatever's under that veil? I haven't asked for a new surprise any more than she has.

I decide to distract myself with a little food and make to grab one of Lillian's famous buns—only to find the table littered with strange foods. I drop my hand back to my lap and study the various dishes.

The foods have a distinctive Asian feel, and Lillian has propped label cards under the more obscure dishes—not that knowing the names helps me decipher if the various plates are actually edible. In front of me, there's a bowl of white rice covered in gooey brown beans. The folded cardboard identifies the dubious recipe as Natto. Next to it, a black plate is elegantly laid with grilled fish—Yakizakana, apparently. Fish for breakfast? Not my thing. The next plate looks even more revolting—a blackish, dried seaweed called Nori. Another greenish salad thingy sits behind it: Kobachi. Then there are green pickles—sorry, Tsukemono—another giant bowl of white rice, and whatever Lillian is brewing on the stove.

My stomach grumbles in hunger and churns in disgust simultaneously. Whatever happened to good, old-fashioned pancakes and bacon for breakfast?

Weary of the various *treats* on display, I end up staring blankly into space while throwing the occasional suspicious side-glance at the veiled shape in the corner. That's when I realize I must look just as frowny and miserable as Marco and Kate did when I walked into the kitchen.

Kate's dad joins us a few minutes later, and soon afterward my parents arrive. Pops Teddy pays the kitchen a visit, but he inspects the table and runs off before Lillian can trap him into joining the unusual breakfast party. He's probably gone to eat something from his secret stash of Bluewater Springs Chocolate sweets that he's not supposed to have but no one has been able to find and confiscate yet.

The only Asian-style breakfast enthusiast is my dad. The moment he steps into the kitchen, he examines all the various *delicacies* on display. He turns a few labels, helps himself to a small spoonful of the gooey beans, and smiles in wonder at Lillian.

"Lilly," he says, "I thought you were giving us just a taste, but you've gone hard-core traditional. And what's that on the stove?"

"Miso soup," Lillian replies.

Poof.

The last chance of having something palatable for breakfast has just disappeared. I've nothing against Japanese food, just not for breakfast. Thank you very much.

"Ah, of course." My dad approaches the cooking range, grabbing a ladle on the way. "Mind if I try it?"

"Please help yourself, Bud." She waits expectantly with a hand on her hip for the verdict.

"Delicious, but I'd add a spoonful of soy sauce."

"You think?" Lillian seems skeptical, so my dad gathers another ladle of soup and carefully adds a single drop of soy sauce from the bottle.

"Try it now," he says, offering the spoon to Lillian.

Kate's mom swirls the hot liquid in her mouth as if she

were tasting wine, and her face brightens.

"You're a genius." She pats my dad's shoulder.

That's the Bud-Lillian team in action, constantly improving and perfecting each other's recipes. They're the secret behind The Bluewater Springs Chocolate Company's success. Alongside the other two parents' business acumen, of course. It's always best to mention both pillars of the company, lest one set of parents get offended.

Anyway, now that the roll call is complete, I feel it's the right time to bring up the subject of the veiled silhouette again. And, hopefully, I can also find out why we're being submitted to this *gourmet* breakfast—not knowing is driving me crazy.

I ask as much, in less sardonic tones.

Lillian gives me a big smile and invites my mom to join her at the head of the island next to the humanoid shape.

"Abigail," she says. "Since this is your accomplishment, would you like to tell the kids?"

Mom beams at her best friend and then launches into her presentation. "As you know, we're expanding to the UK next year. The London facilities are completed and will be open for business soon. But I've also cultivated a little secret side project. I've been searching for a partner in the Asian Market forever, and this year, thanks to the Chucokate, we might finally secure one. So," Mom pauses for effect while my brain frizzes out. Heightened stakes on the Chucokate; just what Kate and I needed. "It is my great pleasure to announce the birth of The Bluewater Springs *Chokorēto Kōjō!*"

And if Chucokate sounded ominous, this sounds even worse.

At our startled and confused expressions, my mom explains, "We're expanding to Japan!" With excessive flare, she removes the veil from the humanoid shape. "You guys are becoming a manga!" She reveals a life-size cartoon poster of me and Kate.

For a moment I'm lost in the art; the drawing is superb and the artist a skilled one. My brain at once buzzes with all the possible merchandise products we could associate with the new manga design. Funkos, mini-figures, maybe even a board game. The possibilities are dizzying.

From across the island, Kate throws me a don't-you-dare-say-it's-cool look, as if she read my mind.

So I keep my mouth shut and stare at my smiling mother, a bit mortified. She knows how much I love this stuff, and she was probably expecting a more enthusiastic reaction.

The smile dies on Mom's face. "Well, the investors will join us tonight to finalize the terms of the deal. A bit unexpected, I know, but once I sent them the Chucokate projections and a few of the shots you kids took with Josiane, they decided to fly in from Japan to meet us in person. So, we're going to bring them out to dinner later, the whole family. And we'd like you guys to give them the deluxe factory tour tomorrow."

I maintain my unresponsive attitude and lower my eyes to the table, unsure what to do with myself. I feel like anything I say will just cause more problems.

Kate takes the lead. "But Mom," she says, and gets promptly interrupted by Lillian.

"I know what you're about to say, Honeybun." I bet she doesn't. "That with the wedding to organize, you already have too much on your plate. But don't worry, I've hired a professional to help us out with the last details. Annika Lowes is the best wedding planner in Michigan, and you won't have anything to do other than meet with the seamstress to take your measurements and discuss the redesign of my dress." Lillian stops to check her watch. "She's coming over at eleven for the first fitting, by the way."

My mom jumps in as well. "And we know we're asking a lot with a baby on the way and the wedding approaching, but our new business partners have a tight schedule and could only come to the United States for a few days before the end of the year."

Kate and I stare at them in astonished silence.

Marco, who has been sitting silently all this time, now turns to Kate and bursts out, "Are you *seriously* not going to say anything?"

Kate stares at him guiltily. "Marco, let's talk about it later."

He stares at Kate, bewildered.

"Is something the matter?" Lillian asks.

"No, Mom," Kate reassures her. "Just a few things to rearrange, that's all."

"But—" Marco begins.

"Later," Kate hisses.

Lillian gives her daughter an odd look, then moves on. "Okay, why don't we all get a taste of our new partners' traditional breakfast, then?" She picks up the gooey beans bowl. "Who wants some Natto?"

Marco stands up. "I apologize, Mrs. Warren, but I'm not feeling very well. I'm going to the barn." He walks out of the kitchen.

Kate scrambles to her feet, saying, "I'd better go check on him." And follows him outside.

Lillian shrugs. "Your friend is too grumpy, Chuck, he's done nothing but scowl since he's arrived. And the way he forces Kate to run for hours every morning is not healthy."

"Tell me about it," I mumble.

Reinvigorated by her clear dislike for Kate's secret boyfriend, I raise my plate and offer to eat the gooey beans. I hope I won't regret this.

"Here you go, Chuck," Lillian says, happily piling beans onto my plate. "You know, Marco didn't have to pretend to be sick to skip breakfast."

Ah, whatever she puts on the table, never refuse Lillian's cooking, or risk ending up on her red list forever.

"*Arigatò,* Lillian," I say with a little wink.

"Oh, Chuck, you're going to be the best son-in-law ever."

At least one of the Warren women still prefers me. Pity it's the wrong one. And I know I should feel sorrier for Kate. But if her sophisticated, mature boyfriend throws a tantrum over what's clearly a business decision, I can't help her.

I mean, can't Marco see we have to keep up the pretense until the investors have gone?

What if he gives Kate an ultimatum? He looks like the douche-y, ultimatum-giving type of guy.

Is she ready to tell him *sayonara?*

Twenty-three

Kate

I excuse myself and run after Marco as he storms out of the kitchen, and then out the front door. The man is going so fast he's already cut halfway across the garden by the time I get on the doorstep. To keep up, I follow without putting on a coat; I'm still wearing slipper boots. But wet toes and potential frostbite are the least of my concerns right now.

"Marco," I yell after him. He doesn't stop, doesn't flinch, and keeps marching toward the barn. I run and gain on him. "Marco, wait!"

He reaches the door, opens it, and slams it shut in my face. Undeterred, I reopen it and follow inside. Marco picks up his rucksack from beside the couch and gets busy stuffing the bag with his clothes.

"What are you doing?" I ask.

"Packing. Isn't it obvious?"

"But why?"

He stares me down. "Because I figured you were about to explain to me how you can't possibly tell your parents that I'm your boyfriend—and not that other spineless amoeba back in the house— now that the investors from Japan are coming. You find reason after reason to put it off, and I'm sick and tired being your dirty little secret."

"Chuck's not spineless," I interrupt. "And neither am I. This is about protecting our family business, Marco. I thought you got that."

"Oh, sure, it's all about business. And it has nothing to do with you still having feelings for the guy you're fake marrying in a couple of days?" He laughs bitterly, and my hackles are instantly raised.

"Chuck and I are *over*, Marco. How many times do I have to tell you that? We weren't compatible anymore."

"Really? Because Bluewater Springs has transformed you into this person I can't recognize. You've let your training slack, you've been eating all kinds of junk food—"

"It's the holidays, Marco. That's what normal people do."

"—and you've gone from being a confident woman to this little girl who's too afraid to confront her parents and tell them the damn truth for once."

"Wow. Just… wow! I'm not claiming to be perfect, but I don't deserve for you to throw cheap judgments in my face. I'm perfectly capable of handling my life."

He raises his eyebrows. "And yet, you still haven't told your parents the truth. Fake wedding's still on, fake baby's still on the way. You're doing a great job of handling your life, Kate. Really stellar."

"I'm going to tell them," I repeat stubbornly, well aware I sound like a broken record.

Marco shoves his running shoes into the sack. "When?"

"The investors will only be here today and tomorrow, so we'll tell our parents tomorrow after the Japanese delegation has gone I pr—"

"You promise, Kate?" he says, throwing my words back at me with a skeptical pout.

"Marco, I'm not going to marry Chuck, okay? We'll give the investors the tour, and then we'll come clean with our families."

"Unless something else comes up."

"Nothing will. I mean, what else could happen at this point?"

"I don't know. Maybe your parents will buy a second house for you and all your fake kids, or make a movie about you and Chuck to go along with the manga, or a reality show. The sky's the limit, right?"

"Don't be ridiculous."

"You call *me* ridiculous when you plan to wait until two days before the wedding to call it off? That's cutting it awfully close, Kate."

"What difference does it make? Why can't you give me another day?"

"Kate, I've been waiting for four months. I'm tired." Marco zips up the bag in two angry pulls. "Let's do it this way. I have a few friends down in Traverse City. I'm going to crash with them. Once you've called off the wedding—*if* you call off the wedding—give me a shout." Rucksack slung over his shoulder, Marco pushes past me toward the barn door.

"But what am I supposed to say, we told everyone you came for the ceremony?"

"I'm sure you won't have any problems coming up with a new lie," he says, making a theatrical exit complete with a slammed door.

A minute later the BMW engine roars to life and tires screech on the iced gravel. He didn't even say goodbye to my family, now everyone is going to hate him forever.

I sag on the barn's couch about ready for a good cry when Pops Teddy plonks down next to me, saying, "I didn't like him much, anyway."

"Pops," I say, while a rush of adrenaline freezes the tears in my eyes. "How long have you been listening?"

He sighs. "The whole time."

"You've heard everything?"

"Yep!"

Great. Just great. Out of the frying pan, into the fire. "Are you mad at me?"

"I'm sorry I'm not going to be a great grandpa after all, but it takes a lot more than a fake wedding and a fake pregnancy to knock me off my game." Pops boxes the air with a one-two punch, making me smile.

"Any advice?"

He chuckles and wraps me in a warm hug. "Sometimes young people are too blind to see what's standing right in front of them."

I blink at him. "Huh?"

Pops pats me on the leg and stands up again. "Sorry, Honeybun, but you'll have to figure this one out on your own. Now, can we go back to the house and see if the Japanese breakfast nightmare is over? I'd like some decent coffee, and they only keep that instant crap out here."

"I'll walk you," I say, standing up as well. "You know, you're not supposed to cross the garden on your own in winter. What if you fell?"

Pops gives me another long stare. "Then I'd get back up and keep walking."

And with that last pearl of wisdom, we make our way back to the house.

The moment we step inside, my mom ambushes me. "Kate, where have you been? The seamstress has already arrived; she's waiting for you in the studio."

"Mom," I say, wishing life had a pause button. "Where's Chuck?"

"Oh, look at her, she can't stay one minute away from her fiancé!" she gushes. "I think he's still in the kitchen with his parents. You'll see him later. Now, studio."

Mom grabs me by the elbow and drags me into Dad's studio. I don't bother protesting. When has that ever helped anything?

For the next half an hour, I let myself be measured while absentmindedly agreeing to everything the seamstress proposes about design upgrades. I mean, I'm never going to wear this dress, or walk down the aisle in it, so who cares?

***

After the dress fitting, I corner Chuck before everyone gathers again for lunch, and drag him up the stairs to my bedroom.

"Marco left," I say without preamble, closing the door behind me.

Chuck takes a minute to digest this news. "Left, as in he's departed from Bluewater Springs, or left, as in he's left *you?*"

"Unclear," I say curtly. That is *so* not what I want to think about right now.

"Are you okay?"

No, I'm not. I haven't been since coming home. And since leaving Pastor Grant's office yesterday, things have only gotten worse. I've been feeling guilty toward Marco for lying to him, for going back on my word, and for all the unresolved feelings for Chuck that have been nagging me from the moment I laid eyes on him again. And I've also been feeling guilty toward Chuck, for forcing him to have to deal with Marco, for picking useless fights with him to keep my distance… and, since his admissions at couple's counseling, for the possibility that I might've broken his heart.

I stare at his concerned face and feel even worse. I've barely talked to him since we left church yesterday, too afraid of what I might ask and what he might answer, and here he is ready to comfort me.

"Chuck, please, there's no need to pretend you're sorry to see him go. The fact that you're not gloating is already enough."

A storm brews in Chuck's eyes, and he closes the distance between us, placing both his hands on my shoulders. "Kate, I am sorry. Before we were… err… together, you were my best friend. I'll always care about you. Whatever upsets you upsets me."

This day has been so horrible, and I'm so tired of feeling like crap all the time, that I'm ready to indulge in a little human contact. So I let myself go and hug Chuck. And, oh gosh, he smells so good, and his body pressed against mine feels so right. I hold him tighter.

He's startled at first, but soon hugs me in return, his hands gently caressing my back.

Alarmingly fast, the scene turns into a replica of *Dawson's Creek*'s most cathartic episode: season six, episode two. Dawson and Joey have a friendly hug in her dorm bedroom, and before long they're making love for the first time.

I bury my face in the nook of Chuck's collarbone and lose myself in the moment. My poor mind, expedited by Chuck's hands moving on me, quickly plunges into a dangerous train of thought. If what Chuck said about the towel test is true, it means he wasn't ignoring me—he really didn't see me. Which means he never stopped wanting me.

And if Marco did dump me today, which I'm pretty sure is what happened, then I'm technically a free woman. And I don't know, living in such proximity with Chuck has made me want to rip his clothes off since the first night we shared my bed. And right now, I can't remember any of the *super valid* reasons why I broke up with him in the first place.

I raise my head and stare into his blue irises. Chuck looks back at me, eyes questioning.

And if my eyes could answer, they'd be shouting: take me, take me now!

Sometimes Chuck is rubbish at reading my mind. But right now he receives the unspoken message loud and clear. He pushes a loose strand of hair behind my ear, leans down, and kisses me.

The kiss is the most tender, yet most passionate, kiss I've ever experienced. The way his lips move against mine encompasses a lifetime of friendship, a ten-year relationship, and the longing of four months spent apart. It all becomes wrapped up in a whirlwind of emotions, unspoken feelings, and regrets.

I don't care if kissing Chuck is wrong. Messy. Unwise. Dangerous. It feels too good to stop.

I want Chuck. I want him now. And I need to get rid of all these layers separating us.

I yank his sweater off, so that our lips only have to be separated for a few seconds. I'm getting started on his belt when the door bangs open and my mom screeches. "Oh, sorry, guys, so sorry. I see you're... err... busy. But lunch is ready, so whenever you want to come downstairs... I mean, I'll go now."

The door clicks shut, and Chuck and I are left staring at each other in an embarrassing, horny, disappointed silence.

The moment is gone. We both know it.

Chuck pulls his gingerbread man sweater back on and, with a cheeky smile, says, "We'd better go downstairs before they start thinking we're trying to add another fake baby to the family."

And that's one of the great things about Chuck. He can make uncomfortable situations not so awkward, take the edge off any crap life throws at us. He's always been able to make me laugh.

In the past four months without him, I might've become a morning person, made a ton of spontaneous trips, attended many mundane events, and discovered plenty of new restaurants, but I haven't laughed as much as I used to. I've missed it.

I've missed him.

***

The rest of the day is a blur. At lunch, I feed my parents a lie about Marco having to go help a friend with a family emergency. Nobody seems too grief-stricken by his premature departure; all they care about is making sure we're ready to receive our prospective Japanese partners.

The delegation lands in Detroit mid-morning and arrives in Bluewater Springs mid-afternoon. And after a quick stop at the hotel for our guests to freshen up, the dads go pick them up and escort them to the restaurant.

Throughout the meal, I pay little attention to what's being said. I'm too busy eye-flirting with Chuck from across the table. The fake engagement has brought us closer, retransforming us into that boy and girl that used to do everything together. And we have unfinished business from this afternoon. I can't wait for dinner to be over, and to ship Mr. Tagawa Yoshiaki & Co back to their hotel so Chuck and I can pick up where we left off.

Soon, we're going to be alone in my bedroom and nothing and no one will keep my hands off Chuck tonight.

But, like everything else on this holiday break so far, things never go according to plan.

The hotel the Japanese are staying at is a block away from the restaurant, so even total newbies can't get lost. In fact, they opt to walk back while the rest of us head toward the parking lot.

Chuck and I rush to my parents' car, both eager to get home and—I'm hoping—under the sheets. But then Abigail calls out, "Chuck, you're with us tonight."

"What do you mean, Mom?"

Abigail smiles embarrassedly. "I know it's a little old-fashioned, but we thought it best if you didn't sleep with your bride-to-be so close to the wedding."

He looks like she knocked the floor out from under his feet. "Why?"

"Tradition. The groom shouldn't see the bride the night before the wedding."

"The wedding isn't for another two days," Chuck protests.

"Nonetheless, you should abstain from, uh, certain things before the ceremony."

Ah. So my mom must've told everyone Chuck and I were about to screw each other's brain senseless in my room earlier—which we were totally about to, to be fair—and the parental conclave must've established that hot, premarital sex is not appropriate all of a sudden.

This is medieval tyranny, plain and simple, and with the worst possible timing. And the most frustrating thing is that, a week ago, I wouldn't have had a problem with it at all. I probably would have welcomed it. But now…

I stare at Chuck and read the same frustration in his eyes.

Yep, tonight would've been the mother of all sexy nights.

But maybe it wasn't in the cards. Better this way. We don't need any more confusion in our lives, and a night of hot, steamy sex wouldn't have helped to keep our heads straight.

I walk up to Chuck and give him a soft kiss on the cheek. "Good night, Chuck."

"Night, Kate."

Twenty-four

Chuck

Alone in my room, I stare at the ceiling in a state of total confusion and despair, alongside the obvious sexual frustration.

I've prayed for days to have just a few quiet hours by myself. To be at home, away from all the drama. And the *one* night I want to spend at Kate's, it figures I'd end up alone in my bed instead. Be careful what you wish for, right?

Also, what happened today in her room? What did the kiss mean?

I know what it meant to me, and that I started it, but for her? Kate seemed eager enough… but then, she'd just broken up with Marco. Am I nothing more than the rebound guy?

The ceiling doesn't hold any answers for me, no matter how long I stare at it. I wish I had the nerve to call Kate and ask her directly… although I'm not sure she'd have any more answers than I do.

Still, for the first time in a long while, I'm looking forward to seeing her tomorrow.

***

The next morning we meet directly at the chocolate factory and, among all the investors and parents, we can't talk alone. Also, we have a job to do.

We step into the roles of tour guides easily, since we've chaperoned this tour together so many times it's a well-practiced routine. Once all the investors have gathered in the main hall—a big, circular space with wide glass walls and revolving entrance doors—Kate steps in and begins the spiel.

"*Konnichiwa,* everyone," she says. "I'm afraid that's the extent of my Japanese." The delegation responds with demure, close-lipped smiles. Guess this won't be our most hot-blooded audience, but Kate and I can work any crowd. "Thank you for joining us today on this tour of The Bluewater Springs Chocolate Factory," she continues, unfazed by the lukewarm response. "Before we move into the actual factory, I wanted to tell you a little more about what we're going to learn on today's tour. What is chocolate, the ingredients chocolate is made of, how chocolate is made and molded into different shapes, and why it became such a popular treat as soon as it was discovered."

The Japanese all bow and nod, apparently satisfied with the morning's agenda.

It's my turn, so I step forward and clear my throat to draw their attention.

"What is chocolate, you might wonder. Many of us eat it without thinking what chocolate is made of—which, in most cases, is a mix of cocoa mass, sugar, and other ingredients like powdered milk." I point at the explanatory panel behind my shoulders. "But why do we need all these ingredients? Well, we do because the cocoa is extremely bitter when eaten in its raw state. In fact, the name 'chocolate' comes from the Aztec word *xocolatl*, which means bitter water."

At this point, I sometimes tell a joke on how 'bitter water' may sound bad, but it's nothing compared to what the Aztecs called avocados—*āhuacatl,* or, in plain English, testicles. Something about the texture and shape and the way they grow in pairs inspired the unflattering name. The pun usually kills, but I don't think this group would appreciate that particular brand of humor. So, I move on with the regular presentation.

"The most unique ingredient is, of course, the cocoa mass, which is made from the seeds of the cacao trees." As I speak, I catch Kate's eye and find her struggling not to laugh. She knows I've skipped the T-joke, and now we probably both have the T-word stuck on repeat in our brains. I look away, suppressing a smile and trying to keep a poker face as I continue with the standard introduction. "And it's with these tiny seeds that everything starts. If you'd like to follow us, we can now move to our sorting facility."

We guide the visitors through our chocolate-making process, from bean sorting, to roasting, to cracking and winnowing—to get rid of the outer husk of the cocoa beans—to melanging with the other ingredients, and finally to the tempering stage which allows the chocolate to cool down in a controlled environment allowing for only tiny, uniform crystals to form as it solidifies. It's an impressive operation we've built here, and the Japanese delegates seem pleased.

Then we move on to the chocolate bar production facility and show them how the chocolate is molded, shaken to remove any air bubbles, and chilled to create bars. The final stage of the process is packaging, and we watch as the chocolate bars move along the conveyor belt to be wrapped in aluminum foil, then paper, and be finally put into boxes ready to be shipped to the stores.

All throughout the visit, Kate and I are completely in sync. We finish each other's sentences, never miss a beat, and even manage to snatch a smile or two out of the serious boss-man Mr. Tagawa Yoshiaki.

We're one hell of a team. Always have been.

When the tour is over, I'm positive our new partners are going to leave Bluewater Springs impressed.

In fact, Mr. Tagawa Yoshiaki bows to us saying, "I had been told the two of you were the best possible faces for The Bluewater Springs *Chokorēto Kōjō,* and I now agree. The Chucokate will be a big hit in our country." Then he bows, adding, "*Otsukaresama deshita.*"

"*Deshita,*" Kate and I reply, with no idea of what we're saying.

The Japanese leave to continue the business talks with Mick and my mom, leaving Kate and me finally alone.

"So," Kate says. "That went well."

"Our best tour in a while, I'd say."

"What now?" Kate shifts on her feet. "We wait for the Japanese to leave, and then we gather our parents and tell them the truth?"

I'm about to reply, when my world suddenly goes dark. Something rough has been pulled over my head—a sack? As I panic, Kate lets out a little scream. Are they after her too? I flail out with my fists, hoping to catch one of our attackers unawares, but hands grab me and prevent me from struggling free.

A million possibilities cross my head, each one less likely than the next. I'm being kidnapped for ransom. Marco and his gym buddies have come to teach me a lesson about fake-impregnating other dudes' girlfriends. The Yakuza has followed Mr. Tagawa Yoshiaki and they want in on the deal and aren't going to say *please.*

I redouble my efforts to struggle free, but whoever is holding me is strong and doesn't budge.

"What's going on?" Kate asks. Her voice is surprised, but not nearly as panicked as it should be, if members of Japan's most notorious crime syndicate were actually abducting us.

If a response is given, I can't hear it. Someone slides a hand in my pocket and takes out my phone. Something heavy—a blanket, perhaps—is wrapped tightly around me.

Another point against the Yakuza theory. The Japanese mafia wouldn't worry about me catching a cold.

Once I've been turned into a human burrito I'm bodily lifted off my feet. The guy holding me from under my armpits gets someone to help him and lift my legs. They carry me away in this awkward, gangly fashion until we stop again outside. Even wrapped in the heavy blanket, I can feel the dramatic temperature change from the cozy, chocolaty warmth of the factory to the crisp air of a sunny winter day.

Whoever has taken me dumps me in what I assume must be the back of a car or a van. Yep, the seats soon begin vibrating underneath me as the engine shudders to life and the car is put into gear. Gravel screeches under the tires as they drive me away to who knows where.

Twenty-five

Kate

Five minutes earlier...

Chuck and I have barely finished congratulating each other on another successful tour when Finn, Gary, and Phil appear out of nowhere, fast as lightning. I yelp in surprise as Phil pulls a black sack over Chuck's head and then grips my fake fiancé by the shoulders, preventing him from moving.

"What's going on?" I ask, while Gary steals Chuck's phone from his pocket, hands it over to Finn, and then wraps a heavy blanket around Chuck. Chuck flails wildly, but the guys quickly get him under control.

"Surprise bachelor party," Finn whispers in my ear, as Gary lifts Chuck's legs and together with Phil, they carry him away.

"What?" I protest. "Where are you taking him? For how long?"

"That's classified." Finn shrugs. "Can't tell you."

"But I need to talk to him."

"It's going to have to wait," he says, pointedly switching Chuck's phone off. "Sorry, no cell phones allowed where we're going."

He makes it sound like they're about to embark on a *The Hangover* style mega bachelor party—what happens in Vegas stays in Vegas, and all that. When in reality, they're probably going to some D&D retreat in the woods where they'll dress up in chainmail and go full medieval on me with their crap about no tech allowed.

Which Chuck would love, to be fair, but the timing couldn't be more wrong. "Finn, you don't understand. I *need* Chuck here."

"Kate, I respect that, really." He places a patronizing hand on my shoulder. "We all love you and recognize that, starting Friday, you're going to be boss. But tonight and tomorrow are Chuck's last nights of freedom, and we, as his best friends, are honor-bound to make sure he has a blast."

With a wink, he lets my shoulder go and jogs a little backward, still holding Chuck's phone hostage. "I don't think you'll have much time to miss him anyway. You've got your own fun coming."

Finn jerks his chin at the glass front doors, outside of which a pink limousine is pulling up. A few of my oldest friends tumble out of the limousine, waving pink and white cheerleader pom-poms above their heads that match the magenta tutus they're wearing over their winter clothes.

While I'm distracted by the cheering, Finn turns around and runs away.

Then the pink swarm is on me. I'm smothered in hugs and carried over to the limousine and, without doubt, my own surprise bachelorette party.

***

A few hours later, I'm sitting in my living room sipping a virgin Rossini surrounded by diaper cakes, baby monitors, and tiny rompers—turns out mine was more of a surprise baby shower than a bachelorette party. Outwardly, I'm smiling and laughing and having the best time of my life. Inwardly, I'm cursing the day my fake baby won't be born.

At least Chuck will be able to get drunk at his party, they *had* wine in the middle ages. But I have to rot on my couch, drinking strawberry juice mixed with zero-alcohol Prosecco, and listen stone-cold sober to parenting advice I don't need.

I drop my glass on the coffee table, and something squeaks under my bum—a rubber duck. One of the many toys that have been gifted to my nonexistent baby today. I dig a few more toys out from under me and add them to the pile of gifts that will join the miserable stack of wedding presents slash Christmas rejects already stored in my bedroom.

"Don't worry, Katy," my cousin Gretchen says, probably picking up on my dejected mood. "Today has been all about the baby, but tomorrow is all for Mommy!"

An icy shiver sneaks down my spine. "But tomorrow is the day before the wedding!"

"Exactly," Gretchen says, grinning. "And what better way to get ready than with a full day at the spa? We've booked you a facial, a full-body wax, a mani-pedi, and of course a pregnancy massage. It'll be a blast."

That actually sounds pretty great—except for the full-body wax, perhaps. But as much as I would love a spa day, tomorrow's the last day that Chuck and I have to put a stop to this madness. I doubt there'll be much time for mani-pedis. I'm taking a rain check on the pampering—I hope the spa appointment can be postponed, I'll sure need it after talking to my parents. Or I could give it to my mom instead… sorry, Mom, no wedding and no grandchild on the way, but here's a recycled spa gift certificate for you.

"Thank you, girls," I say. "But Chuck and I are busy tomorrow—"

"No, you're not," Sarah, one of my oldest friends and Phil's girlfriend, says. "The boys won't be back until late at night."

I feel like I might faint. "How late? Where did they go?"

Sarah shrugs. "No idea. The guys made this secret man-pact and refused to tell any outsiders. But don't worry, I made Phil promise Chuck would have enough time to recover before the wedding, and he swore they wouldn't get a stripper."

Ah. Perhaps they're not playing Dungeons and Dragons in some shack in the woods after all. But it really doesn't matter what they're doing, as long as they come back in one piece. There's no way I'm telling our parents by myself, and tomorrow's our last chance.

I don't like to admit it, but Marco was right. Life keeps getting in the way. We should've told them the first night we arrived home—or, hell, back in September when the breakup actually happened. Our families would have had four months to get over it before we saw them face to face. But now we're down to the wire, Chuck is gone, and I tried his phone half a dozen times already, but it always goes straight to voicemail.

I'm going to have to deal with this myself, aren't I?

No. I refuse. This is a two-person mess, and it should have a two-person solution. Chuck must be as desperate to talk to me as I am to him; maybe he'll find a way to steal his phone back from the guys. I'll just have to keep calling him until he picks up. Then, we can decide what to do together.

Twenty-six

Chuck

…

I can't remember anything from the past twenty-four hours…

…

I need to sleep…

…

I might be sick…

…

I'm never touching a drop of alcohol ever again…

…

Twenty-seven

Kate

Eight o'clock on Thursday night, and Chuck's phone is still off. I've texted Sarah, and she's assured me the guys all got back in one piece an hour ago. So why hasn't he called me?

I could drop by his house and check in person. But if I told my parents what I was up to, Mom would freak out and insist the bride and groom shouldn't see each other the night before the wedding. As if a little bad luck could stop this wedding from happening; at this point, even the Goddess of Fortune herself would be powerless to stop it. The universe seems intent on getting Chuck and me to walk down that aisle, come hell or high water.

And even if I lied to my parents and went to Chuck's house, Abigail wouldn't let me through the door for the same superstitious reason. An in-person visit is out of the question.

Of course, I could always just walk downstairs and confess everything. But the idea makes my skin crawl. The thought of the look of hurt in my parents' eyes, the disappointment...

So you're going to get married tomorrow just so you don't upset your parents? a little voice asks in my head.

I stare at the cellophane-covered white dress hanging outside my closet.

What is it going to be, to confess or to walk down the aisle?

Neither option sounds good, and anyway, I shouldn't decide alone.

The only other sensible thing to do is to try Chuck's home

number. Even the night before the wedding *talking* to my fake fiancé is allowed, isn't it?

Abigail picks up on the fourth ring. "Hello?"

"Oh, hi, Abigail, it's Kate. Is Chuck there, by any chance?"

"Hello, Darling, yep, he got home an hour ago and went straight to bed. The guys made him party pretty hard last night, I suspect."

"Could you still please put him on the phone, I really need to talk to him."

"Everything all right, Darling?"

"Yeah, yeah, sure. I just want to"—I quickly search my brain for a plausible excuse—"hear his voice real quick." I make a silent mock gag at my corniness.

"You two young turtle-doves, you're too cute," Abigail coos. "Just a second, Darling, I'm on the kitchen's phone. Let me go grab the cordless in the studio."

The line clicks, then silence, then shuffling noises as Abigail meanders through the house. She knocks on Chuck's door and gets in, I hear them battle as she tries to wake him up, and he groans and tells her to go away.

Until, finally, a sluggish, groggy Chuck speaks into the phone. "Hullo."

"Chuck!" I yell. "What are you doing?"

"Please keep your voice down." I can practically see him lift the phone away from his ear as he winces. "My head is killing me."

"Oh, I'm so sorry I'm inconveniencing you, but in case you've forgotten, we were supposed to tell our parents about us *yesterday* before you ran off to do heaven knows what with your friends."

"Hey, I was kidnapped. I had no choice."

"Yeah, okay, whatever. I hope while you were busy getting wasted you came up with a plan, because unless you really want to get married tomorrow, we have to do *something*."

"Kate, I have a splitting headache, I only slept an hour last night, and I'm still hungover. I need to sleep it off."

Typical Chuck. Irresponsible and inactive.

"Fine," I snap. "Guess I'll see you at the altar, then. I'll be the one in white."

Okay, maybe I can be a *little* passive-aggressive from time to time. But can you blame me? Look what I have to put up with!

"If you don't want to come just run off, brides do it all the time."

"Yeah, so you can play the victim while the entire town paints me as the villain. Why don't *you* run away?"

"Okay," Chuck says.

I blink. "What do you mean, *okay?*"

"I won't show tomorrow, all right? No groom, no wedding."

"Are you being serious?"

"As a migraine. Which I currently have. Can I *please* sleep now?"

Not a perfect solution, but if Chuck doesn't show at the church, I won't have to walk down the aisle. Our parents will have to come up with a believable excuse to get rid of the guests. And once the waters settle, we'll be able to explain everything to our families. Okay, sure, the canceled wedding will remain the gossip of the century in town, but at this point, it would have, anyway.

"All right, Chuck. Let's do it your way. Guess I won't see you tomorrow."

He doesn’t reply. Instead, a sound that suspiciously resembles snoring comes through the line. He must’ve already fallen back asleep.

Twenty-eight

Kate

On the day of my non-wedding, I wake up almost cheerful. Today, finally, the nightmare will be over.

I dress up and pamper up as if this actually were my wedding day. I get my hair professionally styled, my makeup done, and pull on the dress, which turned out a lot better than I could have ever imagined.

The puffy sleeves have been subdued into fitted long sleeves, and I'm channeling all the right Kate Middleton vibes. I'm wearing boots instead of fancy shoes, and my lace sleeves aren't see-through, but it's winter. Adjustments had to be made.

I raise my skirts and look at the pretty knee-length, round-point white leather boots. These are the only accessory I remember picking out of the entire outfit. They're warm, practical, and the heel is not too high.

Pity no one will get to see them. At least, not today.

I sit on my bed and take a couple of selfies. My face hasn't looked this good in, well… ever. The makeup artist was a contouring master, and if it hadn't taken her an hour to create her masterpiece, I'd learn how to contour myself.

I'm still making silly faces at my phone when my mom barges into the room.

"Kate, why are you hiding up here? And don't sit on the bed, you're going to wrinkle your skirt. Come on, we have to move or we'll be late. Everyone is at the church already."

"Everyone?" I ask, as a tingle of dread rises up my arms and gives me goose bumps. "All the guests, you mean."

"The guests, the pastor, your fiancé. Everyone."

"Chuck's there?" I squawk.

Mom gives me a weird look. "Of course. Where else would he be? It's his wedding, too. In fact, he's been welcoming guests for half the morning. Annika says everything is ready to go—we just need you."

Annika is the wedding planner Mom hired.

I try to keep a straight face as my heart threatens to explode out of my chest and go cower in a dark corner. What now? What is Chuck playing at?

Last night, he promised he wouldn't show today. What's he doing at the church? Was yesterday's promise a trick?

He's totally reversed gears on me, and now that the groom is present, the only alternative is that *I* bail. But I can't bring myself to do it. I'm no Julia Roberts. I can't pull off the runaway bride act and live with everybody in town hating me forever.

Oh, he must think he's being so clever.

Think again, buddy. You're not turning me into the bad guy.

I'm going to call Chuck's bluff like it's no one's business.

I grab the white faux-fur jacket—the final piece of my outfit—from its stand on the wall and let Mom help me put it on. Then I gather my skirts and exit the room. "Come on, Mom, let's go."

***

Twenty minutes later, as my dad makes the last turn on the dwindling uphill road that leads to the church and parks on the cobbled plaza in front of the chapel, I don't feel so smug anymore.

Dad's black Cadillac SUV, like everything else, got a

complete makeover today. The florist came to the house earlier and decorated the car with white ribbons and a flower piece on the hood that forced us to drive at ten miles per hour to reach St. James, allowing me to experience all the various stages of panic during the slow journey: anxiety, cold fear, jitters, hysterics. And now, as we get out, hot sweats—even if outside the temperature is flirting with the below thirties.

Luckily, the wedding planner suggested a traditional entrance for the bride, where all the guests are gathered inside the chapel, and only the photographer and Josiane Masson—when did she even get back?—are waiting for me outside.

Mom gives me one last tearful, quick hug and then sneaks into the church to take her seat in the front row.

Soon, it's only Dad and me. And our devoted photography team, of course.

He offers me his elbow with a proud smile that fills me with shame. "Shall we?"

I swallow and take his arm. As if on cue, *Everything Has Changed* by Taylor Swift ft. Ed Sheeran begins to play inside the church.

Who chose this song?

It must have been Chuck. *Everything Has Changed* has been our song since the first time we saw the video of the two best friend kids destined to fall in love. We might've been those kids.

But I surely didn't tell anyone to play this song as I walked down the aisle, because I never planned to walk down the aisle. Why did Chuck request this song? Has this been his plan all along—to win me back by tricking me into marrying him?

I know I sound crazy. But really. It's *our song*. Just

hearing it brings on a wave of … even more confused feelings.

I'm petrified, I can't move. But Dad gives me a gentle push and prompts me forward as we make our grand entry into the church. The setting, the music, the flowers are all very grandiose and romantic.

And the damn song! It carries so many wonderful, tender memories; it's really hard to stay cool or remain indifferent. My poor heart is suffering too many contrasting emotions—fear, regret, longing, even love, maybe—to know what to do with itself. It's pulsing in my chest in an agitated beat, making it hard to focus on anything but my own two feet.

Then I lift my gaze and meet Chuck's eyes for the first time. The palpitations don't improve—quite the contrary.

The groom is devastatingly handsome in his black suit and with his hair combed back. Chuck's face is still on the pale side—he's probably not fully recovered from the past days' revelries—but then, the Gentleman Vampire look always suited him.

Once our eyes lock, they stay together. I don't know what either of us is thinking. My head is exploding with all the reasons I should turn around and run for my life. Except, bizarrely, my heartbeat has ceased its frantic racing. That stupid organ is watching Chuck, and it likes what it sees. It could be the song, or the fact that Chuck's eyes have never looked bluer. Whatever it is, warmth spreads from my heart all the way up to the tips of my ears and down to the tips of my toes.

The walk to the altar is both too long and over too soon. When my dad finally hands me over to Chuck, my feelings aren't any more sorted. For an instant, Chuck and I stand in front of each other, transfixed. But then the rational part of me takes over, and I pretend-hug the groom so I can whisper in his ear, “What are you doing here?”

Chuck tries to pull back, but I hold on tight, so he can’t escape.

“What do you mean, what am I doing here?” he hisses.

I ignore how intoxicating his cologne is. “You were supposed to bail on the wedding. You promised last night.”

“Kate, I haven’t seen you for two days.”

“No, but we talked last night over the phone, and you—”

“No, we didn’t.”

He sounds so certain. Oh, gosh. He must’ve still been too drunk to remember our conversation. What now?

Pastor Grant loudly clears his throat behind us. “Now, now, kids, you’ll have the rest of your lives to catch up,” he says, prompting a few guests to chuckle.

Chuck and I pull apart and take our places at the altar, because what else are we supposed to do? Everyone we know and love is sitting there in the audience, staring up at us with happiness and anticipation. I have no idea what is about to happen. But it looks a lot like we’re about to get married.

“Dearly beloved,” Pastor Grant intones. “We’re gathered here today in the presence of family and friends to join this man and this woman in matrimony. In the years they’ve been a couple, their love and understanding of each other has grown and matured, and now Chuck and Kate have decided to live their lives together as husband and wife.”

The pastor pauses for air, and I realize what’s about to come next. My one last chance at coming out of this church unwed. “Now, before we proceed. If any person present has a reason this couple may not be joined in matrimony, let them speak now or forever hold their peace.”

A long pause ensues, and we all look around waiting to

see if anyone will speak. I have a fleeting fantasy that Marco will burst through the doors and challenge the marriage, giving me the perfect opportunity to make a run for it… but no, he's nowhere to be seen.

Should *I* speak? Am I allowed to object to my own wedding? Chuck looks like he might say something, but then he presses his lips tightly together and keeps his mouth shut.

I'm not sure what I was expecting. For the ceiling to split open and lightning to incinerate us, maybe, or for the floor to swallow us and carry us to hell, where we surely deserve to be for all the lies we've told. Or back to my Marco fantasy—except for some reason this time he bursts into the church riding a horse, probably to make the moment more dramatic. But none of that happens—and when I glance desperately at Pops Teddy, hoping that he'll say something since he's the only one who knows the truth, he just gives me a supportive smile.

The deafening silence rings in my ears as I stand there, stunned, while no one speaks up. The moment passes and goes, leaving Pastor Grant free to carry on with the ceremony.

"Please join hands," he instructs us. Turning toward Chuck, he asks, "Do you, Chuck, take Kate to be your lawfully wedded wife, promising to love and cherish her, through joy and sorrow, sickness and health, and whatever challenges life may throw at you, for as long as you both shall live?"

Chuck's hands are cold and clammy. Is he freaking out as much as I am? He stares at me in silence for a long time, as if fighting an internal struggle.

After a while, Pastor Grant coughs. "Err, Chuck, do you?"

Chuck blinks at the pastor, looking lost, as if he didn't

know where he is or what he's doing. Then he looks back at me, squeezes my hands, and, giving me a cryptic wink, turns toward the congregation.

"I'm sorry, but I don't," he announces.

A shocked, collective gasp rises from the audience.

Still holding my hands, he looks at me and, in a clear voice, says, "Kate, nothing would make me happier than to become your husband, but not today, not like this."

He lets go of one of my hands and, keeping the other for support, I assume, turns to face the audience. "The truth is that Kate and I broke up months ago." Another dismayed gasp shakes the crowd. "In fact, Kate has a new boyfriend. His name is Marco. He's half Cuban, a professor of Latin Art, and he likes to run. Like, a *lot*."

My face and neck flame in embarrassment. Elbowing him with my free arm, I hiss, "We don't need to be *that* specific, Chuck."

He just grins, the jerk. The smile quickly fades as he turns to face our parents. "Mom, Dad, Lillian, Mick… We know how much you loved the idea of us getting married, and for our families to finally become one. That's why Kate and I didn't have the heart to tell you we'd split up. Instead, we kept lying to you for months, pretending we still lived together. We came home prepared to tell the truth, but then you told us about the Chucokate and the entire campaign you had planned around us as a couple, and we didn't know what to do. And then Nana Fern gave me the ring, and I was showing it to Kate and it fell to the floor, and I got on one knee to pick it up, and that's when you walked through the door, Lillian, and assumed I was proposing to Kate, so I did, and Kate was forced to say yes."

Our parents' jaws—along with every other jaw in the

room—have dropped so low I'm surprised they haven't dislocated. It's hard to blame them—it's a hell of a truth bomb to drop on anyone, especially at a wedding.

Mom recovers first. "So… it was all a lie?"

"I'm afraid so," I say.

"But what about baby Margot?"

"There's no baby, Mom. You overheard us talking about the breakup and must've heard wrong. When you confronted me and asked for a different explanation for a secret that was making me sick to my stomach I should've said it was lying to you all, but I didn't."

"We swear we wanted to come clean the next day," Chuck continues, "but we didn't want to ruin our last Christmas together."

"Then the day after the entire town brought presents," I take over.

"And then you bought us a surprise house," Chuck says.

"And then the Japanese investors came."

"And then the ambush bachelor party happened."

"And then…" I stop, realizing I've run out of and-thens. "I know it sounds like a pile of excuses, but I swear, we tried to tell you a million times."

My mother's eyes are watering. She looks devastated. So, basically, the exact thing I've been trying so hard to avoid.

"And you felt the right time to come clean was at your wedding?" she says faintly.

"We were scared," Chuck blurts. "You put so much pressure on us, on our relationship—did you even think to ask us about the Chucokate campaign before barging ahead with it? We didn't know how to tell you. We didn't want to disappoint you. And, in short…" He takes a deep breath. "That's why we can't get married today."

Dead silence in the church. Someone coughs, and it feels as loud as a gunshot.

Well, that went terribly. Time to make a graceless exit. I squeeze Chuck's hand as I say, "Thank you for coming. Sorry for how it turned out. Now, if you'll excuse us…"

Time to run away from our own wedding.

Twenty-nine

Chuck

Kate squeezes my hand and drags me out of the church at a run before anyone can react. We stop at the massive wooden front doors and let go of each other's hands to push them open in a collective effort. And we're out.

Only Mick's Cadillac is parked outside, as per the church's strict no-parking-except-for-the-bride's-car policy. But we don't have the keys.

What now? I'm lost, but Kate grabs my hand again and drags me down the narrow pedestrian pathway that leads into town. In her white fur and low-heeled boots, she's the perfect winter runaway bride. But without my coat, I'm the will-freeze-to-death-soon runaway groom companion. I'm wearing only a suit, and December in northern Michigan should not be tackled without, at minimum, a parka.

I'm about to tell Kate how ridiculous this escape is, that we don't need to run away. The worst part is over. We came clean. We should go back and enjoy the reception with our friends and families. We'll call it a New Year's Eve party instead of a wedding celebration, and after a few drinks, no one will care. But then I turn my gaze toward the church doors, I see our parents standing on the steps, staring after us. The dads are mostly astonished, but the moms have murder in their eyes.

Guess the parents are not ready to be philosophical about the whole canceled wedding business. I wonder if they're madder at the public embarrassment, the forsaken dreams of a Warren-Rose dynasty, or the derailed Chucokate campaign. Probably a bit of all three.

No matter the answer, going back is not an option. The view of the four parents of the apocalypse spurs me forward and I manage to keep up with Kate even though I haven't been training for a half-marathon. Another hundred yards, and we tumble off the cobbled church road onto the main concrete street below.

In the distance, up the hill, a car engine roars to life. They're taking Mick's Cadillac to chase us. We need to get out of here fast.

A bus is approaching from the left and, without thinking, I jump in the middle of the road, waving my hands.

Either the bus stops, or I'm dead. At this point, I'll take either.

It's close, but the bulky gray vehicle screeches to a halt a few inches shy of splattering me on the concrete. The driver, visibly shaken even through the windshield, rolls down his window and yells at me. "Are you crazy?"

"Sorry," I say. "But this is a life or death situation."

"Please, help us," Kate says.

Her wedding dress does the trick. The driver's expression quickly changes from anger to shock to curiosity, and he asks, "What happened to you two?"

"No time to explain," Kate says. "But could you please give us a ride?"

"Where are you going?"

"It doesn't matter," I reply. "Anywhere. As long as we leave right now."

The driver stares at us another second, then shakes his head amused. "Sure. Jump in."

He opens the bus doors.

Kate and I mutter a stream of thank yous and head for the

open doors. Kate's in front of me and climbs the first two steps without trouble, but as she reaches the double doors her skirt gets stuck in the entrance.

"Hurry," I say, looking behind my shoulder as Mick's black Cadillac takes the last turn downhill before the main road. They're gaining on us.

"Help me instead of complaining," Kate protests. "Can't you see I'm stuck?"

I gather all the skirts and underskirts in my arms and push Kate forward until she explodes into the bus in a white tulle bomb. I pull myself up after her, then beat my hand on the console. "Go, go, go!"

We pull away and sprint down the road just as the Cadillac comes to a stop at the crossroads.

I tear my eyes from the window and have a first look at the inside of the bus and its passengers.

From the twin rows of seats lining the bus, at least twenty pairs of young, shocked eyes stare up at me. We've crashed a Girl Scout bus!

Kate and I stumble to the middle of the coach until we find two empty seats and sit down nonchalantly as if it were perfectly normal to go around in wedding clothes hijacking strangers' buses.

I've just about caught my breath when a mad honking behind us makes me jump again. It's our parents. They're following us.

"Is there any chance you could speed up a little?" I ask the driver.

"Sorry, pal," he says, looking disapprovingly in the rearview mirror. "But in case you haven't noticed, this is a bus full of kids."

I wince. "Ah. Right."

The two adult troop leaders seated in the front row—a blonde with short hair, and a brunette—turn and scowl at us. Okay, we probably deserve that.

If the girl scouts throw us out, we're toast. So I refrain from making any further requests and hope we'll still manage to lose our parents somehow, despite driving at a lamentably legal speed.

Thankfully, a few miles ahead we pass through a traffic light just as the light switches from green to yellow. Mick has never run a yellow light in his life. In fact, I glance through the rearview window, and rejoice as the black Cadillac promptly stops while we sprint away.

Bye-bye parents.

Kate and I can finally share a sigh of relief. And I know it's completely nerdy, but I lift my hand for a high five. Kate slams her palm right into mine, smiling.

"We've lost them!" she cheers.

We nod at each other, satisfied, and focus ahead to the road and an unknown destination.

A blonde girl with pigtails climbs onto the seat in front of us and turns back to face us. "So, are you going to tell us what happened, or what?"

Thirty

Kate

I stare at Chuck. He shrugs, so I take it upon myself to share the insanity our life has become.

"It all started two weeks ago, when Chuck and I had to come home for the holidays and he rented the wrong car—"

"What was wrong with the car?" a girl interrupts.

"Couldn't fit half my stuff in the tiny trunk."

"I don't think the girls are interested in this level of detail," Chuck cuts in.

"You tell them what happened, then, if you're such a better storyteller," I say.

"Right," Chuck says. "Girls, the story begins two weeks ago, when Kate and I came home for the holidays. *Period.*"

Chuck puts extra emphasis on the last word.

"What's the big deal about coming home for the holidays?" an Asian girl with pin-straight black hair asks. "Everyone does that."

"Ah, but we were carrying a secret with us," Chuck says in a mysterious tone. Guess all the hours spent on role-playing games with his friends gave him augmented narrating skills.

The audience of small girls oooohs at this. And a chorus of questions follows.

"Really?"

"What secret?"

"Who were you keeping it from?"

Chuck sighs. "We'd been hiding the truth from our parents." And, pointing at the back window, he adds, "The ones we just shook off."

"But what was the secret?" a redhead with cheeks covered in tiny freckles insists.

I scoff. "It was that we'd broken up," I say. "Okay?"

A collective gasp echoes through the bus.

"You broke up?" the blonde girl with the pigtails repeats.

"Technically, she dumped my ass," Chuck says.

"I thought we weren't being over precise," I say while another shocked intake of breath shakes the bus.

"He said *ass*," someone whispers, accompanied by a chorus of giggles.

The Girl Scout troop leaders glare at us, and one of them snaps, "Language, young man. This isn't a hooligan bus going to a tailgate party."

"Sorry, Ma'am," Chuck apologizes. "Anyway, we had to share the bad news with our parents, which was no easy task since they're not only best friends but also business partners."

"Wait, wait. Wait," a girl with brown curls interrupts. "You haven't told us why you two broke up."

The blonde girl with pigtails stares at me. "I bet he was being insensitive to your needs," she says in the most natural tone.

"Exactly," I say. "That, and a good deal of other stuff."

"I imagine he never bought you flowers," another girl says.

"No, never," I confirm.

"And that he never surprised you with romantic weekends," another girl adds.

Chuck stares at the girls, dismayed. "Are you all part of some man-hating cult or something? Come on, maybe I wasn't the best boyfriend, but I wasn't *that* bad."

The redhead speaks again. "Boys can be so selfish sometimes."

Pigtails speaks next. "Was he at least any good in bed?"

I almost choke with embarrassment. "Do you know what 'being good in bed' means, Sweetie?" I ask, while the driver not-so-subtly coughs from his position behind the wheel.

"No," Pigtails admits. "But my big sister always asks her friends if their boyfriends are good in bed, so…"

My cheeks flame beetroot red. But, since they have no idea what it means… "He was good in bed," I admit, truthfully.

"Oh, what a relief," Pigtails replies. "My sister says a relationship has no chance of working otherwise."

"Anyway," Chuck says, distinctly hassled. "Let's stay focused on the story, girls. So, we're coming home to tell our parents we've broken up."

One of the girls in the front raises her hand. "Excuse me, sir?"

"Yes?"

"Aren't stories supposed to begin with once upon a time?"

A murmur of agreement spreads across the bus.

Chuck sighs. "Fine, once upon a time two weeks ago, we were coming home for the holidays when—"

"No, no, that's not right," another girl says. "The story has to start before that."

"Where should it start?" I ask.

"How about when the two of you fell in love?" she says, and gives a longing sigh like she's experienced heartbreak the rest of us could only dream of.

Chuck exhales. "Do we really have to—"

"Yes!" they chorus.

He rolls his eyes. "Okay, fine, let's do it your way, girls. Once upon a time, there were a boy and a girl who lived in a chocolate factory…"

I smile as I listen to Chuck tell the story of the little boy and girl who grew up together in a chocolate factory and would get into all sorts of trouble. Like that time they wanted to pull a prank on everyone and switched sugar with salt in the factory machines. That's still the official story of how our world-famous salted-caramel bars were born.

"Then the boy and the girl grew up, and they eventually moved out of the chocolate factory," Chuck continues. "But they always remained friends, and they kept getting in trouble together for many years. Until they fell in love, and on a cold winter night they kissed for the first time."

The girls all giggle in approval, except for one girl who puts her hands over her ears, saying, "I don't want to hear the rest of the story."

"Why not, Sweetie?" I ask.

"Because if the prince and the princess don't live happily ever after, I don't want to know."

"Ah," Chuck says. "But the ending of this story hasn't been written yet." Then, looking around the bus, he asks, "Who wants to hear about the cruel king who tries to steal the princess away?"

"Me!"

"Me!"

"Me!" the girls chorus.

"Seriously?" I ask flatly.

Chuck grins. "Gotta give the people what they want."

I roll my eyes but let him move on with the story—if nothing else, for the entertainment of our little saviors. "The evil king's name was Marco…" Chuck intones, and the girls all lean forward in anticipation.

Marco comes out of Chuck's narration a little worse for wear, as he tells the girls everything—the various misunderstandings, Marco's surprise visit, the fake baby—until Chuck reaches the end and gets to the part about our dramatic confession and subsequent flight from the church.

Our young audience is hypnotized. Entranced. A few girls are gazing at Chuck as if he really was the prince in a fairytale—and I have to say, dressed in his best suit and groomed to perfection with his blue-black hair drawn back, it's easy to believe he could be a prince who's leaped off the pages of a storybook.

A brunette with a short fringe has a different reaction, however. She stands up and walks back a few rows to go hug Chuck.

"Hey, what's up?" he says, patting her back. "You okay?"

She cups his ear with one hand and whispers something in a slow murmur so that only he can hear. Then they exchange a look. Chuck nods sadly and ruffles her bangs. She hugs him again, kisses him on the cheek, and goes back to her seat.

I stare at him with my eyebrows raised. Chuck waves me off, like it's nothing.

But it's not nothing. Chuck wasn't just telling them our story—he was telling it from *his* perspective. And while most of it was what I experienced, some of the things he said, particularly whenever he was talking about how things used to be with us…

An incredible sense of loss is weighing on my chest. And, if I'm being honest, it has been oppressing me since Chuck came to pick me up in the Nissan Versa ten days ago. I wasn't ready for the avalanche of emotions seeing him again unleashed in me. That's probably why I picked a huge fight with him right off the bat—to fuel my anger, to remind myself why we didn't function as a couple. But the more time we've spent together, the more we've had to work as a team. Until today and this final, ridiculous escape in a Girl Scouts bus.

And his words at the church today, *I love you, Kate, and I'd love nothing more than to marry you one day, but not today, not like this.*

In the rush of the moment, I didn't have time to process what he said. But now that we've stopped for a moment, I can't help but wonder again. Is Chuck still in love with me?

And what about me? What do I feel for him?

I look over at him, and there goes the now-familiar ball of warmth that spreads from my belly to my chest, reaching up to my cheeks. Well, if gut reactions are to be taken as any kind of sign, I'd say I'm pretty screwed.

My reverie is interrupted by Pigtails. She leans against the backrest and looks me straight in the eyes. "May I ask you something, Princess Kate?"

"Sure," I say.

"Was the cruel King Marco any good in bed?"

My cheeks flame even redder, and I dare a side-glance at Chuck.

He, too, turns toward me. "Please don't answer that."

Thirty-one

Chuck

We stay in the Girl Scouts bus for close to an hour. I have no idea if our parents are still following us or not, but as the driver pulls into a camping ground near the coast, I'm pretty sure it's time for a reality check.

"Girls, be quiet now, we've reached our campsite," one of the troop leaders sitting in the front calls out. "Let's assemble in the clubhouse until I have the keys to your lodges. We'll grab your luggage later, all right?"

Cheers erupt from all over the bus, and the girls dismount in a surprisingly orderly fashion for kids so young.

Kate and I wait for the last girl to leave before we exit ourselves. It's still early afternoon, but the sun is already making a quick descent over Lake Michigan.

Kate stares at me. "What do we do now?"

I give her a twenty-dollar bill. "Go to the clubhouse and see if they have any hot chocolate. I'll come in right after you."

Once she's gone, making more than a few heads turn as she passes other guests of the lodge in her wedding gown, I take my phone out of the inner pocket of my suit and compose a quick text:

The wedding didn't happen, please come pick Kate up

My heart fights in my chest as my thumb hovers over the Send button. Then I clench my jaw, strengthen my resolve, and send the message along with our location.

Once she's gone, I don't know what I'll do. Probably text my parents and ask them to give me a lift back to Bluewater Springs. I'm their only child, and even if I've majorly disappointed them today, they're still bound to love me unconditionally. I mean, they're the two people in the world whose job is to love me and support me no matter how bad I mess up. And this time, I'll admit it was pretty bad.

A chilly gust of wind prompts me to go join Kate inside the lodge. On the way in, I bump into the blonde troop leader.

"Hey," she says. "I forgot about you guys. Are you going to be okay?"

She warmed up to us considerably after hearing our story.

"Yeah," I say truthfully. "The only way from here is up, trust me. Thanks again for the ride."

I find the runaway bride seated at a table near the windows; she's hard to miss in her puffy white wedding gown. Kate picked a pretty nook made of wood-framed tempered glass that overlooks the lake on one side, and the entrance gates and a portion of the parking lot on the other. Similar nooks line the entire side wall.

Kate has taken off her fur, which now lays sprawled on the booth seat, and she's cradling a red mug in her hands. She's turned away from me, looking out the window with her elbows resting on the windowsill, lost in thought.

"Hey," I say, slipping in next to her and twisting so I can enjoy the view. A red mug identical to hers is waiting for me, with white and light-blue tiny marshmallows floating on the surface of the steaming chocolate.

I grab the mug and raise it in a mock toast. "What a day."

I take a sip and can't help but wince.

"Yep," Kate says. "They only have Hogs Chocolate. Can you believe it? So close to Bluewater Springs, and they buy their chocolate from Hogs."

At the mention of our most fierce regional competitor for the Midwest, I fake-bristle.

"Unacceptable. I'll have to speak to the manager before we take off."

"How are we going to leave?" Kate sighs. "Do you have enough cash to pay for a ride back? I don't even have my phone." She bitter-chuckles. "Brides are not supposed to carry a purse."

"Don't worry," I say. "I've taken care of everything."

This earns me a small smile.

When Kate finishes her drink, she sets the mug down and stares at her left hand. Slowly, she removes Nana Fern's ring from her finger and hands it to me.

"Well, at least now the charade is over."

The tiny slip of metal weighs a ton in my palm. As if Kate just handed back to me the last ten years of our lives along with the ring.

"It wasn't all bad, though, right?" I say.

"No," Kate says, and looks away.

We sit in silence for a long while afterward. Until the roar of a sports car makes us look toward the entrance, where a red BMW is pulling up in the parking lot. By now the sun has dropped low behind the horizon, and artificial glittery lights illuminate the outside patio and bare trees.

Marco climbs out of the BMW and looks around uncertainly.

Kate's head snaps toward me. "What did you do?"

"I texted him."

With an unreadable expression, she pulls on her fur and rushes outside to meet him.

They stand beside the patio, which is awash in the warm

light of an overhead streetlight and the intermittent glow of all the fairy lights decorations. The girl scouts sure picked a romantic location for the reunion of Princess Kate and the cruel King Marco.

I should probably go order myself a stiff drink and leave them to it. But I can't tear my eyes away from the couple. They talk for a while; Kate is fumbling with her arms all over the place like she does whenever she's nervous. Then he takes her hands into his as she keeps talking. And then they embrace.

PDAs is where I draw a firm line in the snow, because if I have to watch them kiss, I might actually puke. Doing the right thing sucks. But Kate's made it clear she doesn't want to be with me, and she and Marco only broke it off because of our ridiculous charade. I figure it's up to me to set things right. If Kate loves Marco, they should be together.

I force my gaze away from the window and fixate on the emptiness ahead of me. Blurred lines melt into blurred lights before my eyes.

I'm self-hypnotizing with the hazy dark browns of the wooden furniture and warm yellow glare of the lamps, trying to anesthetize the pain, when a cloud of white invades my field of vision, and my gaze refocuses on Kate as she makes a second spectacular entrance into the lodge.

It's hard to do anything in half measures while wearing a wedding dress.

She all but runs toward me and stops in front of the table, breathless.

"What are you still doing here?" I ask. "Where's Marco?"

"He's gone," Kate says, scooting into the booth.

Bemused, I shuffle over to make room for her. "Why?"

Kate ignores my question completely. "What did that girl

whisper in your ear, earlier on the bus when you finished the story?"

For a moment I'm tempted to say nothing again. But what the hell, why not answer truthfully? I mean, what have I to lose at this point. "She told me she was sorry."

"Why was she sorry?"

"Because she said it was obvious Prince Chuck was still in love with Princess Kate, and it made her sad that they couldn't be together."

Kate's eyes glitter in the suffused lights of the lodge. "And is he? Still in love with her, I mean."

"Yes," I say simply.

"Good," Kate says. "Because Princess Kate has finally realized she still loves him, too."

I grin like an idiot. "And who said the prince and the princess have to get married to have a happily ever after?"

Thirty-two

Kate

Chuck pushes a loose lock of hair behind my ear. "Want to know something else funny?"

"Always."

"Do you realize what day today is?" he asks.

"The day we ran away from our own wedding?"

Chuck laughs. "Besides that. Technically, it's our tenth anniversary. Remember New Year's Eve? Aspen?"

"How could I ever forget?"

That Christmas, my dad had gotten into his head that he should learn how to ski and convinced the entire gang to go to Colorado for the holidays. Our parents rented a beautiful cabin in the woods and, while no one actually learned how to ski—Dad was the most tenacious, but gave up after three days, declaring the task impossible—it was a great vacation full of scenic walks in the forest, sleigh rides, and delicious food.

On New Year's Eve, we were all playing a game of Risk during which Chuck and I got eliminated spectacularly fast. So while our parents finished the game, we decided to go wait for the New Year on the roof of the cabin, figuring we'd have a better view of the fireworks from up there.

The night was clear and bitterly cold. Chuck and I changed into full mountain wear and, all puffy and clumsy, we climbed out the window and cleared a patch of snow to sit on the roof, snuggling close together under a heavy wool blanket.

At the stroke of midnight, fireworks exploded all around

us, and we looked into each other's eyes, neither of us speaking as if we both just knew. That was the first time we kissed.

Now, ten years later, Chuck is staring at me with the same wonder I saw in his blue eyes all those years ago. And when he kisses me, I swear I see fireworks again.

Gosh, I hope this lodge has a few vacancies left because I have two weeks' worth of pent-up sexual tension to let free.

Chuck breaks the kiss all too soon and takes my hands into his.

"I know we're not getting married today. But would it be okay if we still exchanged vows?"

"Vows? What do you mean?"

"I never want to lose you again, Kate. From this day forward, I vow to come to boring vernissages of modern art neither of us understands with you whenever you want."

I smile. "In that case, I vow to come to the next Star Whatever movie premiere in full cosplay."

"I vow to have sex with you every time you come anywhere near me wearing a towel," Chuck says, making me laugh. "Or, you know, whenever you feel like ravaging me since I'm so good in bed apparently..."

My cheeks flush a little, which is ridiculous considering how many times he's seen me naked. Not in a while, though, but hopefully soon.

"I vow to never assume I know best, and to always talk things through with you," I say, a bit breathlessly.

Circling his thumb over my hand, Chuck says, "I vow to take you on romantic breaks at least once a month, homework-permitting."

"I vow never ever to complain again about you not being a morning person." No more pre-dawn runs for me, thank you very much. I'll run at a civilized time on my own schedule.

Chuck laughs, then turns deadly serious. "I vow to come to London with you next year and stay in the UK for as long you want."

Tears well in my eyes. "Oh, Chuck, would you, really?"

He nods solemnly. "I've given it a lot of thought. London is a great city for design. I could learn a ton there, and I can still work for the company from the UK offices. My job is location-independent, anyway. And besides, how are we going to visit every landmark on your giant list if I'm on the wrong continent?"

"We don't have to visit *every* landmark," I protest.

He kisses me again. "Kate, you were right. I was being lazy, wanting to move back home as soon as we graduated. It was comfortable, and safe. But we only live once, and I want to see it all, Kate. I want to see it all with you."

I hug him and hold on tightly.

"Thank you," I say, half-giggling, half joy-crying. "Turns out Pastor Grant's premarital course wasn't such a waste of time after all. We're pros at handling conflict now. We've sorted out all our issues…"

"Well…" Chuck looks at me with a cheeky grin. "All except for one."

"Which one?"

"How to tell our parents we're back together!"

Note from the Author

Dear Reader,

I hope you enjoyed *Fool Me Twice.* This is the first book in the Christmas Romantic Comedy series, but it doesn't really matter if you started reading here or not, as all books in this series are complete standalones, totally unrelated to each other. Well, except that they share the same heartwarming, fuzzy holiday spirit. I hope you'll want to give the other books in the series a try as well.

The "next" book in the series is a modern-day retelling of *A Christmas Carol.* My reimagined Scrooge is Caroline, a career woman who gave up on love and the chance to have a family to pursue her dream job. But when a cheeky Christmas spirit visits her in the dead of night and brings her on a tour of Christmases that are, have been, will be, and—most importantly—could've been, Caroline will embark on a journey of self-discovery that will bring her to question the past seven years of her life and all the things she's given up to be where she is now.

Now, I have to ask you a favor. If you loved my story, **please leave a review** on Goodreads, your favorite retailer's website, or wherever you like to post reviews (your blog, your Facebook wall, your bedroom wall, in a text to your best friend…). Reviews are the best gift you can give to an author, and word of mouth is the most powerful means of book discovery.

Thank you for your constant support!
Camilla, x

CAMILLA
ISLEY
A
Christmas
Caroline

A Christmas Caroline

Caroline is a cynic career woman living the high life in Manhattan where love and relationships are but a distant memory of the past.

But after a freak accident on Christmas Eve, Caroline receives a visit from a cheeky spirit of Christmas Past, Present, Yet to Come, and—most importantly—Christmas That Could Have Been. When she wakes up on Christmas Day suddenly married with three kids and living two doors down from her parents in New Jersey, Caroline has a chance to experience the life she would've had if she'd made a different choice.

Will small-town life as a mother and a wife make her rediscover what's really important in life?

Acknowledgments

Thank you to Rachel Gilbey for organizing the blog tour for this book and to all the book bloggers who participated. I love being part of your community.

Thank you to my street team, and to all of you who leave book reviews. They're so appreciated.

Thank you to all my readers. Without your constant support, I wouldn't keep pushing through the blank pages.

Thank you to my editors and proofreaders, Michelle Proulx, Helen Baggott, and Jennifer Harris for making my writing the best it could be.

And lastly, thank you to my family and friends for your constant encouragement.

Cover Image Credit: Created by Freepik

Lightning Source UK Ltd.
Milton Keynes UK
UKHW011950021221
394964UK00002B/413